Year '57

A

Book by

Ashraf Jamal
(*Author of* ***Mahout***)

Editing: Arbia Khalid
Cover: Tapashi Sen

Introduction

This story has been built with bricks of imagination on the foundation of true events of our first war of independence. Its primary objective is to illuminate the often-overlooked sacrifices of lesser-known revolutionaries from that era, their contributions having been obscured by various historical factors. By envisioning the emotions, endeavors, and sacrifices of the ordinary people of that period, this story endeavors to breathe life into their struggle. It stands as a testament to our rich culture and illustrious history, representing the convergence of diverse streams of knowledge within our nation. Beyond merely recounting the actions of both male and female leaders, this story also unveils the untold tales of women who bore the brunt of hardship behind the veil. It aspires to bridge the divide that has arisen among the offspring of Mother India, a pressing necessity in our nation today.

"If you are killed in battle, you will attain heaven, and if you win, you will enjoy the kingdom of the earth. Therefore, O son of Kunti, stand up with determination for the battle." - **Bhagavad Gita 2.37.**

Hindostan ….

The land of ancient dynasties witnessed a myriad of legacies. From the Shakas and Kushanas to the Rajputs, Pallavas, Chalukyas, Cholas, Mauryas, Guptas, Pathans, Hindi Turks, Marathas and Mughals, some were integrated into this land through sacred fire on its rivers' ghats, while others found their resting place within its soil. Then, across seven seas, arrived the British, intent on plucking the feathers of this golden bird over a span of 200 years. As they sank their claws deep into the motherland's chest, her children could no longer bear the pain. They set aside their discord and disputes and sounded the trumpet heralding Hindostan's first war of independence. Leading the way was the venerable patriarch, Emperor Bahadur Shah Zafar, the last heir to the throne where Hindus, Muslims, and individuals of all faiths could stand in unity beneath a single roof, carrying the torch of this revolutionary movement.

A few years before the rebellion of 1857 -

On the route from Lucknow to Shahjahanpur, there exists a small village. The evening has arrived, and the sun, weary after a day's labor, is poised to descend below the horizon. Its brilliant reddish glow has enveloped the fields in a soft, velvety pink, casting the path that winds through the fields in the likeness of a long, slumbering white serpent. Moving in the direction of the village were two individuals: the village's Imam, Abdur-Rahman, and Kabir, a lively 16-year-old youth with dusky skin and a mischievous glimmer in his eyes. Imam Sahab, a robust and self-assured figure, possessed a rugged physique and radiated an aura of devotion and wisdom on his forehead and visage. He was attired in a white labada and adorned with a saffron turban atop his head. Today, Imam Sahab found himself slightly delayed for Maghrib's prayer as he spent some extra time in his laboratory, situated outside the village. Observing the reddish hue of the sky, Imam Sahab gauged the time and began to speak –

"Son Kabir, it seems we won't be able to reach the village in time for the Maghrib's call to prayer. However, we are fortunate that I had informed Pandit Ramdas about our schedule today. He for sure will send someone to the mosque to make the call to prayer (Azaan)."

"Yes, ustaad ji" - Kabir nodded in agreement with the Imam Sahab's words.

Pandit Ramdas, too, had a moderate stature, a muscular physique, and an unmistakable radiance of wisdom and erudition gracing his countenance. His intelligence shone so brilliantly that even a person without sight could perceive it. After a wordless stroll covering some distance, Imam Sahab placed his hand upon Kabir's head with a sense of pride and remarked -

"You produced acid today with such skill and caution, using the lessons from the past, I am proud of you, my son." - Imam Sahab said, placing his hand on Kabir's shoulder.

"What lesson did you learn from Pandit ji this week?" - Imam Sahab asked, still keeping his hand on Kabir's shoulder.

"I was taught trigonometry by Pandit ji and he also made me practice it thoroughly. Now, I can measure the height of any object easily from a distance. I understand all the aspects and calculations of parallax, and to some extent, I can even calculate how the object will move in the air depending on its velocity if it's thrown from a certain angle." - Kabir told everything in one breath.

Imam Sahab, showing his surprise with affection, widened his eyes and said - "Okay...SSSS!"

Imam Sahab chuckled softly as he grabbed Kabir's earlobes and teasingly asked - "That's all good, but why did you put a frog in Pandit Ji's coat? He was so angry. Someday, he will subject you to such a beating that you'll remember it for the rest of your life, you little troublemaker!"

"Ow! Ow! He makes me work too much and beats me if I make a mistake." - Kabir explained with pain in his voice, clarifying his position.

Imam Sahab released Kabir's ears and put his hand on his shoulder to explain – "You won't find a mathematician and calculation expert like Pandit Ji anywhere in India. So, my boy, learn as much as you can from him. You are fortunate to have been born on this land with a passion for learning and acquiring knowledge."

"How can anyone be fortunate just by being born on a certain land?" - Kabir expressed his disagreement.

Imam Sahab started answering solemnly- "Come on! Let me give you a brief history lesson. Hindostan was the first country to show the world, the light of knowledge and technology. Esteemed scholars such as Bhaskar, Aryabhata, and Brahmagupta excelled in the fields of mathematics and computation. In addition to these luminaries, Varahamihir, alongside numerous Hindu, Buddhist, and Jain scholars, contributed new perspectives and principles. It was in Hindostan where the world learned the meaning of zero and infinity. The astronomers here were the first to measure the movement of stars. Charak made Ayurveda and surgery popular, and there was no one in the world who could match the metallurgy of Hindostan. After the sixth century, when this golden era ended, the knowledge was spread to the Islamic world through Arab merchants, which led to the beginning of the Islamic golden age."

Imam Sahab paused for a moment and then continued - "The Islamic society combined Greek and Indian knowledge together, likened to pearls on a string, making it practical and easy to use. The introduction of papermaking techniques from China, via Arab traders, facilitated the rapid dissemination of knowledge. Scholars such as Abdullah Ibn Mu'adh Al-Jayyani in trigonometry, Khwarizmi in algebra, Al-Kindi in chemistry, and Hasan Ibn Al-Haytham in optics expanded the dimensions of knowledge and gave these subjects new heights with new theorems, inventions and discoveries. Additionally, Al-Biruni and numerous other scholars made groundbreaking discoveries and inventions in mechanics. Many of the today's machines we are familiar with and these firangis possess can trace their origins back to that golden era. In the realm of alchemy, a method or formula was developed to transform even iron into gold by integrating techniques from Indian, Arabic, and Chinese traditions. Although Muslims had resided in India since the 6th century, it was only when the Turkish, Afghan, and Mughal empires established themselves in India that the Indian and Islamic branches of knowledge converged, much like two seas meeting, colliding on the surface but giving rise to novel creations beneath. The Turks, Afghans, and Mughals settled in India, leaving an indelible mark. Indian civilization and culture took on a new form known as 'Indo-Islamic,' which is still evident today."

After saying so much, Imam Sahab took a deep breath and said - "So my son! It is a great fortune to be born on this land and to have the eagerness and zeal to acquire knowledge."

Kabir thought for a moment and then revealed the question boiling inside him - "Ustaad ji! (thinking deeply), if we were already so advanced in knowledge and technology, then why are these firangis (foreigners) ruling over us?"

The lines of pride vanished from Imam Sahab's face, and instead, sadness and disappointment took their place.

Imam Sahab - "You've posed a profoundly significant question, my child. The root of this issue lies in our lack of awareness, misunderstandings, negativity, and a somewhat naive conviction of our superiority. Up until the reign of Emperor Aurangzeb, the Mughal dynasty stood firm. The sun of India ascended from Delhi, casting its radiance across the entire nation. We led the world in trade and commerce, with Europeans eagerly seeking opportunities to engage with us. Our network of factories spanned the nation, exporting goods to distant lands. Our urban centers and rural communities embraced cutting-edge technology of the era, including watermills, Persian wheels, canals, spinning wheels, and modern handlooms. Our jewelry craftsmanship was admired throughout Europe. Even in military technology, we had no rivals. The quality of our cannon and firearm production exceeded that of the Portuguese and British. Notably, we manufactured Zamburak, a lightweight camel-mounted cannon, superior to even Turkish equivalents. In numerous battles, Emperor Aurangzeb effectively deployed Zamburak to great advantage."

Imam Sahab started speaking in a loud and passionate voice, then slowed down and softened his tone as he continued - “However, Emperor Aurangzeb departed from the alliance established by his predecessor, Akbar the Great. In his narrow-mindedness, he renounced the policy of reconciliation, known as "sulah-kul," which had preserved unity in Hindostan. This decision resulted in not only the oppression and injustice against Hindus but also impacted Sufis, Shias, and other Muslim communities, except those adhering to a strict and dogmatic mindset. Rebellions erupted in various regions. Emperor Aurangzeb, being a military strategist, managed to maintain the empire's coherence and strength during his rule. However, following his era, the empire began to experience increasing instability. A succession of inept and morally corrupt emperors assumed power, leading to the disintegration of the central government. There was a moment when it appeared that the Marathas, successors of the courageous and visionary Chhatrapati Shivaji Maharaj, might exert dominance and restore order in Hindostan. Yet, after Peshwa Bajirao the First, the primary focus of Maratha leaders became revenue collection, without establishing a new system or implementing reforms. Moreover, we fell behind in military technology, and Ahmad Shah Abdali defeated the Marathas at Panipat, using the same old Zamburak."

Imam Sahab said while clearing his throat - "The cause of a nation's downfall is not solely political, my child. The inhabitants play a substantial role in it as well. As the populace is, so are the leaders they get. When the wave of knowledge and technology made its way to Europe through the Ottoman (Turkish) Empire, Europeans made significant advancements. Novel innovations, machinery, and fresh perspectives became widespread. Europe witnessed the establishment of new kinds of factories and the formation of modern weaponry and armies. In contrast, we, the people of India, clung to our traditional knowledge, intoxicated by our own sense of grandeur. We remained oblivious to global developments and failed to incorporate technical knowledge into our Gurukuls and Madrasas, while firangis raced ahead, outpacing us. In such circumstances, their ascendancy over us was practically inevitable. Hence, my child, remember to seek knowledge from all sources, including firangis."

Kabir was listening carefully and understanding everything.

Kabir - "Yes, Ustaad ji. So, was there not a single ruler in our country who could understand these conditions and adopt new military technologies?"

Imam Sahab - "That's not accurate, my dear! Figures like Mahadji Scindia, Maharaja Ranjit Singh, and Sher-e-Mysore Tipu

Sultan embraced innovative military strategies and tactics during their reigns. They trained their armies in the European style and introduced modern approaches. Mysore, for instance, established factories employing cutting-edge technology and brought Chinese experts to enhance silk production, adopting advanced farming techniques. To strike fear into the British on the battlefield, Sultan developed a novel iron cased rocket known as the "Thunder Bolt/Taghrak," which rained down like fire upon the British forces. Even Arthur Wellesley, who later defeated Napoleon at Waterloo, felt humbled by Tipu Sultan's army near the Srirangapatna mound, living in perpetual dread of Sultan's Thunder Bolts. In the northern regions, Mahadji Scindia consistently delivered heavy blows to the British, defeating them in numerous encounters. The reputation of Mahadji's European-style trained army was so formidable that merely hearing his name led many British officers to abandon the battlefield. Regrettably, owing to the absence of a robust central authority, most of our kings, nawabs, and sardars continued their internal conflicts and engaged in senseless warfare. Mahadji and Sultan even contemplated forming an alliance to oust the British from the country. However,

Mahadji's time ran out, and Sultan paid the ultimate price for the treachery of Mir Sadiq, losing his life."

They were on the verge of reaching the village. Ahead of them stood a small grove of trees, and beyond that, the hamlet began, marked by a scattering of dilapidated huts. Both Kabir and Imam Sahab were fatigued, yet as they caught sight of the village ahead, a renewed energy infused their steps.

"Ah! We have finally arrived," - exclaimed Imam Sahab with a sparkle in his eyes.

As they ventured beyond the narrow alley and passed the dilapidated huts, they were suddenly met with deafening sounds. In a moment of foreboding, Imam Sahab seized Kabir's hand and swiftly brought him inside an old yet robust hut. From there, they peered through a concealed window to avoid detection. Through the window, they could clearly see the neem tree where Pandit Ji, Kabir, and Imam Sahab's homes stood. However, their hearts sank as they beheld a grim scene before them: a British platoon led by Officer Reagan was assaulting Kabir's mother, Jasoda, while her husband, Nandu, lay nearby on the ground and pleaded for mercy, but to no avail. The ruthless soldiers continued their brutal assault. Kabir's eyes were brimming with tears and his face was contorted with pain, anguish and fury. He attempted to break free from Imam Sahab's grasp to rescue his loved ones, but Imam Sahab clung to him tightly and embraced him as tears streamed down his beard. He said to Kabir with a firm tone filled with passion, anger, and sorrow, while trying to compose himself,

Imam Sahab -"Son, there will be accountability for every injustice, every single one of them. But if you yourself are not alive, who will hold those demons accountable?"

Kabir's body went limp and he made no effort to escape. He held onto Imam Sahab's kurta tightly, sobbing softly, and helplessly watching everything. Imam Sahab's face showed lines of helplessness. Reagan kept kicking Jasoda's stomach with hatred causing her to contort in agony. Reagan then moved forward and kicked Nandu repeatedly causing him to scream in pain and plead, "Forgive us, my Lord, we won't do it again."

Reagan (in excessive hatred and anger) - "Bloody Indians, where do you get the audacity as pests to not follow the company's order. How dare you defy our orders?"

In the village, the entire population stood frozen, resembling statues, their anxious eyes fixed on the unfolding scene. Pandit Ramdas alternated between rushing to implore the officer for clemency and appealing to Zalim Singh, the village landlord, who was seated close by.

Pandit Ramdas (nervous, helpless, and desperate) - "My Lord! please stop now, they both will die. Please forgive them and persuade Gora sahab to have mercy. Oh my God, have mercy! (pleading to his God)."

Zalim Singh (with a smug expression on his face) - "When the government has ordered that no Hindostani will run a factory, no clothes will be woven, then why should any disobedience be tolerated?"

Pandit Ramdas (stuttering) - "She's a madwoman, please forgive her this time! I'll make her understand the order, they made a mistake."

Zalim Singh (with a crooked smile) - "So why haven't you helped her understand yet,

Pandit? It's not a mistake, it's rebellion! And her punishment will be such that it serves as an example."

Without seeing any kind of hearing, Pandit Ji grabbed the foot of the English officer.

Pandit ji - "Gora Sahab! Please forgive her, spare her life."

Reagan rained blows on Pandit ji's back and kicked him away with a push. The British soldiers did not spare Pandit ji either, and when he fell unconscious, they left him lying in the dirt.

Reagan showcased his cruelty towards Jasoda, relentlessly assaulting her until he could no longer continue. He then summoned the officer, who stood at a short distance, bearing a resemblance to an executioner.

Reagan (with a proud look on his face) - "Gomez! This woman will pay for the defiance, chop off all her fingers."

Zalim Singh remained seated on the cot, exuding the same air of haughtiness. A group of soldiers forcibly moved Jasoda toward a nearby smooth stone, extending her hand flat against its surface. Goms menacingly raised his sword, with the intent of severing Jasoda's fingers. However, Nandu's response was swift, akin to a spear, striking Goms and driving him back. Nandu forcefully pushed Goms away, connecting his shoulder with Goms's abdomen, summoning his last reserves of strength to protect his wife. Within Reagan, it felt as though a fire had been ignited. He swiftly retrieved the pistol holstered at his waist. With precise aim, he fired a shot, the bullet passed through piercing Nandu's forehead. Nandu's lifeless body fell to the ground, much like a broken branch, casting an eerie silence over the entire scene. Even Zalim Singh, whose face had earlier displayed arrogance, now bore an expression of astonishment. The idea that Reagan would resort to shooting Nandu had been completely unforeseen by Zalim Singh. He held the assurance that Reagan would subject them to the same punishment of hand or finger amputation that the company had consistently imposed on the craftsmen and weavers in this region. Ever since foreign powers assumed control over this land, they enforced regulations that barred local craftsmen, weavers, and factories from selling their products within Hindostan. These restrictions resulted in the decline of local manufacturing and trade. Any craftsman or weaver who dared to defy this order faced the grim consequence of having their thumb or fingers severed.

Reagan, along with his soldiers, began to depart. Zalim Singh also rose from his seat with a faint smile gracing his face. However, Reagan's demeanor took a sinister turn. He abruptly turned back, reached for the pistol hanging from Gom's waist, and aimed it at Jasoda, firing a shot that struck her forehead. Reagan's cruelty had already pushed Kabir to his limits, but witnessing him take the lives of both his parents was a devastating blow. Kabir crumpled to the ground, losing consciousness, his heart shattered. Imam Sahab cradled Kabir's head in his lap, seated on the unforgiving floor of the hut, presenting a picture of helplessness and desolation.

♣♣♣♣

In Kabir's life, a tempest had swept through, imprinting his countenance with emotions of "anger," "helplessness," and "smoldering vengeance" in his eyes. On the banks of a small river just beyond the village, the funeral pyres of his parents blazed. Neighbors and villagers, consumed by sorrow and grief, gathered around the biers. Kabir stood amidst them, his eyes brimming with tears, teeth clenched in fury. On one shoulder, Pandit ji placed a consoling hand, while Imam Sahab, clutching prayer beads, stood on the other side. Both the elderly men appeared lost in contemplation of the vast expanse of the sky.

Imam Sahab and Pandit Ji were deeply absorbed in the poignant scene as Kabir's biological father, Abdullah, drew his final breaths. Back then, Kabir was merely an infant, taking his tentative first steps in life. Sadly, Kabir's mother had perished during childbirth, and it wasn't long before the relentless grip of an incurable illness claimed Abdullah's life as well.

♣♣♣♣

Abdullah lay unwell on a cot within his humble hut, with Imam Sahab and Pandit Ji seated nearby, each immersed in their own contemplation of their deities. Jasoda,

Abdullah's god-sister, tenderly massaged warm oil onto his chest, endeavoring to alleviate his discomfort.

Abdullah (sick, panting, and coughing) - "Aapa! Please take care of Kabir after I'm gone."

Jasoda (nervously) - "What are you saying, pagla! Nandu has gone to get Vaidya ji, it's just a bad time for your health, you'll get well soon."

Abdullah (speaking with all his strength) - "Kabir has never seen Fatima, he has seen only you since childhood. Become mother Jasoda to my Kanhaiya, Aapa."

Jasoda (with a choked throat and teary eyes) - "Paagal! You are asking me to become the mother of my own beloved child? Perhaps! God did not bless us with any children so that we can pour all our love onto Kabir."

A faint smile graced Abdullah's countenance as he uttered the Kalima, even as his body grew cold. In response to Jasoda's mournful cries, Kabir, who had been nearby playfully etching patterns in the soil, grew anxious and sought solace by enfolding himself around Jasoda's chest.

Jasoda began to nurtue Kabir with great affection. Nandu would occasionally entertain Kabir by imitating a horse for him to ride, or hoist him onto his shoulders and engage in joyful dance. Jasoda, in turn, would regale Kabir with tales of Krishna's divine Leela, the valor of Hussain, the epic slaying of Ravana and Lord Rama's triumphant conquest of Lanka, or she would narrate the remarkable journey of the Prophet Muhammad during the Me'raj. Kabir was maturing within the embrace of a rich and diverse cultural tapestry.

The morning sun cast its warm glow upon the scene, with Imam Sahab and Pandit Ji comfortably seated on a cot within Jasoda's home, savoring hot puris. Jasoda swiftly served the freshly made puris. In a corner of the house, young Kabir, aged four, crouched with his face hidden, nibbling on a handful of soil. Jasoda, upon spotting Kabir indulging in this peculiar habit, instinctively reached for a pair of tongs with the intent of giving him a disciplinary scolding.

Jasoda (her temper flaring and her face turning crimson) - "How many times have I cautioned you not to eat dirt? This mischievous lad won't mend his ways unless he's reprimanded. Open your mouth, open your mouth!"

Kabir opened his mouth, but even after Jasoda thoroughly checked, she didn't find anything in his mouth.

Jasoda (surprised) - "There is nothing in your mouth! Did you swallow something? (in a stern tone)"

Kabir (stuttering) – "Maa! Did the universe appear in my mouth?

Jasoda chuckled with a fond and gentle demeanor, and her laughter was contagious, drawing smiles from Imam Sahab and Pandit Ji as they were all touched by Kabir's innocence.

These reminiscences moved Imam Sahab and Pandit Ji, their eyes welled with tears. A solitary teardrop traced a path down Imam

Sahab's beard, disappearing into the folds, while one of Pandit Ji's tears descended to the ground, merging with the earth below.

State of Awadh, Bitthoor –

As evening descended, the sun's scorching grip only slightly relented. Its rays cast a brilliant sheen upon the pillars of Nana Sahab Peshwa's mansion, as though they had been meticulously polished with sandpaper. Within the mansion, Nana Sahab Peshwa, akin to a caged lion, paced anxiously in his chamber, awaiting the arrival of his loyal friend and Diwan, Azimullah Khan. Following the Marathas' defeat, the British had exiled Peshwa Baji Rao II to Bithoor and initially provided him with a fixed stipend as a pension. However, after his passing, the British altered their intentions, recognizing Peshwa Baji Rao II's adopted son, Dhondoo Pant, also known as Nana Sahab, as the Peshwa but discontinuing his stipend. In an attempt to reinstate his stipend, Nana Sahab, along with his Diwan and confidant Azimullah Khan, had submitted a request to England. Yet, Nana Sahab harbored little hope of the British displaying benevolence. Azimullah

Khan approached the mansion with swift, purposeful strides.

Upon seeing Azimullah approaching, Nana's face lit up with joy. He advanced towards him with a shout of welcome.

Nana Sahab - "Come, Azim, come! My eyes were yearning to see you. Sit down! You must be tired."

Azimullah Khan settled into one of the chairs thoughtfully arranged within the chamber, and Nana Sahab's restlessness ebbed as he joined his friend. During this interval, a servant, pouring sherbet from a jug, presented it on the table. As Azimullah Khan took a refreshing sip of the sherbet, Nana Sahab posed a grave question in a solemn manner.

Nana Sahab - "What's the news, Azim? I don't even have hope for anything good."

Azimullah Khan - "You are correct, Nana. The British government has declined to reinstate your stipend, deeming it an internal affair of the company. Furthermore, the company's officers exhibit no willingness to entertain the matter."

Nana Sahab (with sorrow in his eyes) - "I do not fret for my own sake, Azim, but I cannot avert my gaze from the plight of the Bithoor's populace. Despite being a constituent of Awadh, Bithoor languishes with each passing day. While Nawab Wajid Ali Shah holds the mantle of Awadh's leadership, the British East India Company exercises dominion, and these profiteers are dismantling not just Bithoor but the entire Awadh and Hindostan. What purpose does the Peshwa's hollow title serve? Had the stipend endured, we could have extended even greater assistance to the people."

Continuing the conversation, Nana Sahab said - "Only a few people are left in the count who still scare the British, and who knows what conspiracies are being hatched to remove them from their path. I am worried about my brave sister Begum Hazrat Mahal. On the other hand, Manu is also surrounded by conspiracies from all sides."

Nana Sahab's concern was visible on his forehead. Azimullah Khan, with a sympathetic tone and a smile, said to ease Nana's worries,

Azimullah Khan - "The British don't fear them for no reason, your sisters are lionesses. Don't worry, I didn't return from England only with disappointment."

Nana Sahab (surprised) - "I don't understand, Azim."

Azimullah Khan - "During my return from England, I made a trip to Turkey. What the Russians did to the Britishers during the Crimean War is worth seeing. If the Russians can do this to these firangis, then why can't we? Why can't we uproot these firangis from our land and sink them into the Indian Ocean?"

Nana Sahab (with a face full of questions) - "Is this possible, Azim? The Russians have armies, weapons, and supplies. Where do we have all of this?"

Azimullah Khan - "We also have an army. How many Englishmen are there in their cantonments, Nana Sahab?"

Nana Sahab - "Why would Indian soldiers in the British army revolt?"

Azimullah Khan - "While they may serve within the British army, British officers hold them in contempt, treating them with cruelty, regardless of their religious affiliation, Hindus or Muslims alike. These foreigners exhibit no hesitation in undermining anyone's faith. The British army's new firearms employ bullets derived from a mixture of cow and pig fat. Restlessness prevails everywhere, Nana Sahab. It is merely a question of time before a collective cry reverberates."

Nana Sahab - "But an army cannot fight without weapons."

Azimullah Khan - "These foreigners have taken over our kings and nawabs' kingdoms, and those who still have their kingdoms, if they do not bow down to the foreigners, their status is no better than puppets. The patriotic rulers will come with us. Those states which have the means will provide us with funds and weapons, Nana Sahab! And there are also some armies with them, we just need to train those armies."

Nana Sahab (smiling) - "It seems like the whole plan has already been prepared! But all these kings and nawabs will need a leader, what do you think about that?"

Azimullah Khan - "The blood of the great Peshwas runs in your veins, who could be better than you to lead?"

Nana Sahab (in a serious tone) - "No, Azim, I cannot. The wounds inflicted by Maratha forces on other states in the past still have not healed. Rajputs, Pathans, Bengalis, and Rohillas will never accept Maratha leadership. Even if they were to agree to accept our leadership, they would not be able to maintain unity among themselves."

Azimullah Khan (in surprise) - "Then who can take up this responsibility?"

Nana Sahab - "The Emperor of Hindostan, Bahadur Shah Zafar."

Azimullah Khan - "But Nana Sahab, he has grown old and is no longer influential. And what guarantee is there that all the kings and nobles will accept his leadership?"

Nana Sahab - "The Mughal Empire remained strong for more than 250 years, and even though it may have diminished today, it still exists. The roots of Sulah-Kul established by Akbar the Great spread across every corner of Hindostan. Emperor Aurangzeb's misguided policies only severed the branches of that tree, but its roots remain strong even today. Remember, Azim! When the Marathas spread across all of Hindostan and held the true reins of power, not a single king, nawab, or Maratha leader declared sovereignty. The allegiance to the emperor remained intact and stayed with the Mughals. The Marathas established their rule, but as deputies or representatives of the Mughals."

Nana Sahab paused for a moment, took a breath, and said - "The East India Company, the looter, has always referred to itself as a mere servant of the Mughal Empire. Do you know the reason, Azim? Because, even then, the emperor, the ruler of all Hindostan for the common people, resided in the Red Fort of Delhi, and even today, he continues to reside in the Red Fort of Delhi."

Azimullah Khan (nodding respectfully) - "Well said, Nana Sahab."

Nana Sahab - "Speaking of Emperor Bahadur Shah Zafar growing old, no matter how old a lion becomes, its roar can still be heard throughout the entire jungle."

Azimullah Khan (in deep thought) - "But the princes of the Red Fort are not worthy enough to endure the hardships of a revolution."

Nana Sahab - "Hmm! You have spoken the truth, Azim. (Reflecting) If the Emperor is safe and sound in Delhi, he himself will address any grievances from the princes. We just need to select an excellent commander for the military command and responsibility in Delhi. The kings, nawabs, and landlords in their respective regions can lead the struggle for independence and as the deputy of Baadshah Salamat, I will raise the banner of the revolution from the fortress of Bithoor."

Azimullah Khan - "For the success of this campaign, one thing is crucial, Nana Sahab: the revolution should begin simultaneously throughout Hindostan so that the Firangis do not get a chance to regroup."

Nana Sahab - "You are right, Azim. We must keep this in mind and also exercise caution so that the firangis remain unaware of it. Whom should we invite to join this revolution?"

Azimullah Khan - "First and foremost, we should extend invitations to your sisters Rani Lakshmibai and Begum Hazrat Mahal

Sahiba. In addition, your comrade and mentor Tatya Tope, Ahmadullah Shah Maulvi, who is one of the finest commanders in Hindostan, Thakur Kunwar Singh, who wields significant influence over the land of Bihar, Sepoy Commander Bakht Khan Ruhela, who can kindle the flames of revolution up to the English barracks, Shah Mal from the Jat region, who can effectively impede the arrival of English reinforcements, Subedar Khan Bahadur Khan from Bareily, Raja Nahar Singh Jat from Ballabhgarh and Badshah Salamat Bahadur Shah Zafar can be invited to join the struggle for independence. Subsequently, we can consider including other patriotic revolutionaries, and the message of revolution can be disseminated to the common people through sufis, ascetics, saints, and sannyasis, thereby uniting everyone in the cause of expelling the English from our nation."

Nana Sahab (laughs heartily) - "You have already made extensive preparations ahead of time. So, let's proceed with the blessings of Lord Ganesha."

Azimullah Khan - "It would be better, Nana Sahab, if you personally meet not only Badshah Salamat but also everyone else."

Nana Sahab - "I'm not feeling well, Azim."

Azimullah Khan (in a state of anxiety) - "What happened, Nana Sahab? You were fine just a while ago!"

Nana Sahab (smiling) - "Write a letter to Company Bahadur, Azim! informing them that for the sake of health benefits, Nana Sahab Peshwa wishes to embark on a pilgrimage."

Nana Sahab and Azimullah Khan burst into laughter, causing their laughter to reach the servants standing at a distance, who were surprised to see Nana Sahab's happiness. After the thunder of their laughter, silence suddenly fell over the atmosphere as Azimullah Khan chose to remain silent immediately.

Nana Sahab (seriously) - "What happened, Azim? Why did you suddenly become silent?"

Azimullah Khan - "I hope that whatever is left in life doesn't get lost in the pursuit of independence."

Nana Sahab ("While placing a comforting hand on Azim's shoulder) - "The Tiger of

Mysore once said before his final battle, 'The life of a tiger for a day is better than a hundred years of a jackal'. Azim, we shall live a day's life of a tiger, just one day."

Hunt –

The village was bordered by a small forest, a habitat for deer and neelgai. Not far from the forest, a spring flowed and merged with other streams. Tall trees surrounded the springs. Colonel Reagan frequently visited the area to hunt animals that came to drink. On that day, he embarked on a quest in search of a deer or neelgai. Reagan sat in a howdah on the elephant, his face filled with pride. When the British first arrived in Hindostan, they were dazzled by its splendor and wealth. Some foreigners began to reside here, attempting to acquire that grandeur and imitate it. As British influence grew in Indian politics after the decline of Mughal rule, British officers saw themselves as kings or nawabs. Reagan, too, with great arrogance, saw himself as a king on the elephant. Some soldiers had rifles slung over their shoulders and swords hanging from their belts around the elephant. Despite waiting a long time, Reagan hadn't managed to make a kill. He was getting frustrated, scanning in every direction when he suddenly saw movement in the tall grass. A gleam appeared in Reagan's eyes, and his hands instinctively adjusted the aim of his gun towards that direction. Reagan was eager to catch a glimpse of the prey beyond the bushes. Suddenly, amidst the bushes, Kabir emerged, holding a bundle of dry sticks. Reagan pulled the trigger of his gun, and the bullet whizzed past Kabir's ear, piercing into a trembling tree trunk. If the bullet had struck an Indian instead of an animal, it wouldn't have mattered to him. But when Kabir emerged instead of an animal, Reagan's aim went astray in surprise. In anger, the red-faced Reagan ordered his soldiers.

Reagan - "Catch this bastard! I will pull his skin alive."

Reagan was frustrated by not being able to find the prey, and he wanted to take out his frustration on Kabir. Sepoys ran towards Kabir to capture him, but when Kabir saw them coming, instead of running towards the village, he jumped into the water and began attempting to cross the stream. Reagan, sitting on the elephant, watched Kabir's desperate attempt to escape. Kabir was swiftly moving through the water, trying to reach the other side. Reagan picked up another loaded gun from the howdah and calmly took aim at Kabir. This time, he didn't want to miss the target. Reagan pulled the trigger, and the bullet bolted to pierce through Kabir's head. However, fate was kind to Kabir that day. As he slipped, his foot gave way, and he stumbled into the water, causing the bullet to pass harmlessly over his head and get lost in the gushing water. Kabir stood up and hurriedly disappeared into the jungle on the other side. The soldiers stood on the edge of the stream missing their chance repenting. When the soldiers returned, Reagan sternly questioned them.

Reagan (looking at the Indian soldiers with a hateful gaze) - "Find him! Who the hell is that bastard?"

A soldier - "I'm not sure, sir, but perhaps he was a village boy from beyond the jungle. We'll find out and let you know, Saahab Bahadur!"

Reagan - "You Indian slaves, worthless, lazy people! you won't amount to anything.

Next time when I see him, I will shoot him in the face."

Delhi, Nizamuddin Auliya's Dargah, 1856 -

In a small room somewhere behind, the atmosphere is filled with the echoes of Qawwalis. Nana Sahab, disguised as a poor Brahmin, Azimullah Khan has taken the appearance of a Dervish, Raja Jai Lal, who was entrusted by Begum Hazrat Mahal, is dressed as a Pathan, Tatya Tope has assumed the attire of a weaver, and Ghaus Khan, the commander of Rani Laxmibai's forces, has taken on the appearance of an East India Company soldier. They all impatiently await the arrival of Emperor Bahadur Shah Zafar, and inside the room, the Dargah's Dervesh, Hafiz Rahmat, quietly enters,

Hafiz Rahmat - "Alampanah Emperor himself is about to grace us with his presence."

Everyone stands up as a sign of respect. Alampanah enters the room along with his servant, Ahmer Beg.

Nana Sahab (smiling with warmth on his face) - "Greetings, Alampanah (joining his hands). May the glory of the Emperor of Hindostan rise."

Bahadur Shah Zafar (with a faint smile on his face, holding Nana's joined hands) - "Why do you embarrass me? Nana! Just call me the helpless King of Delhi, that's enough. Haven't you heard? I am the ruler of the people by the will of God, the sovereign of the nation, and the obedient servant of the Company."

Hafiz Rahmat - "Please don't speak of despair, my Alam Panah! At this moment, the entire Hindostan is looking up to you with hopeful eyes."

Bahadur Shah Zafar - "Please be seated."

Taking a deep breath, the emperor greeted everyone and addressed them.

Bahadur Shah Zafar - "Through Ahmad Beg, your letter reached me Nana and I am aware of your expectations from me.

However, if we want to make this campaign successful, it is better to entrust its reins to the hands of new and young blood. I do not consider myslef worthy of it, nor do I have the age to step onto the battlefield."

Nana Sahab - "If we want to make this campaign successful, it is necessary that you, indeed, take charge of all of us. You are the guiding light, the beacon, whose umbrella shelters us Marathas, Pathans, Rajputs, Jats, Bengalis, Rohillas and the entire population of Hindostan. Together, we can stand united with great zeal and fight for the independence of our nation."

Azimullah Khan - "Speaking of the battlefield, Alampanah, we all will become your arms and together we will drive these firangis out of our land."

Ghaus Khan - "Rani Sahiba has sent her regards to you as a daughter and has requested your leadership."

Raja Jai Lal - "Begum Sahiba and the entire Awadh region have placed their hopes in you, Baadsha Salamat."

Bahadur Shah Zafar - "Whether I lead the struggle for independence or not, in this mission, I will stand together with all of you with my full strength."

Baadshah Salamat Addressing Raja Jai Lal,

Bahadur Shah Zafar - "As soon as I received the news that the Firangis have falsely accused Nawab Wajid Ali Shah of mismanagement in Awadh and have usurped his throne, planning to send him to Calcutta, I sent a message through Hafiz Rahmat Sahab that under no circumstances should Begum Hazrat Mahal leave Awadh. Could this become possible?"

Raja Jai Lal - "Badshah Salamat! When Begum Sahiba brought up this matter before Nawab Sahab, he advised Begum Sahiba to quietly disappear for the sake of the country's independence, even if it meant facing torture and mistreatment from the East India Company for Nawab Sahab. However, this posed a risk of alerting the Britishers to our campaign."

Hafiz Rahmat Khan - "Oh Allah! Has Begum Sahiba gone to Calcutta?"

Raja Jai Lal - "No. Begum Sahiba, after keeping a stone on her heart, openly demanded a Khula (which is a woman's legal right to seek separation from her husband in Islam) from Nawab Sahab and got separated from him. Now, if she is no longer the wife of Nawab Sahab, then on what basis can the English take her to Calcutta?"

Bahadur Shah Zafar (with regret) - "Oh Allah! The daughters of this nation are far superior to the sons."

Zille Subhani composed himself and asked further,

Bahadur Shah Zafar - "Ghaus Khan! How is my brave daughter Manu doing?"

Ghaus Khan - "If the wounded lioness is confined to a cage, how would she be? Badshah Salamat! Rani Sahiba has been restless to wear the saffron turban on her head and she keeps inquiring about your well-being from this slave."

Bahadur Shah Zafar - "Tell Manu that her aged father is now waiting for the moment when the motherland embraces him in her lap, and he meets his Lord. (Addressing Nana Sahab) Watch, Nana! If Manu doesn't sever the ears of these Britishers the most, then my name is not Abu Zafar Sirajuddin."

Nana Sahab (nodding his head) - "Yes, Jahanpanah! she is born to show us all the way."

After a moment of silence, with a slight nervousness and a tone filled with curiosity Baadshah Salamat asked,

Emperor Bahadur Shah Zafar - "Hasn't Scindia been invited to this mission?"

Tatya Tope replied - "No, Alampanah. The invitation for the revolution has only been sent to trusted landlords, kings, and nawabs. And I have started creating small pockets of resistance in Kanpur and the surrounding forests in a covert manner and have begun their training."

Nana Sahab - "In the eastern region, Maulvi Ahmadullah Shah has already taken action to spread the message of revolution to the common people. He has prepared groups of sufis and ascetics and has started sowing the seeds of revolution in every village and city."

Haafiz Rahmat - "The preparations for the struggle for independence in Delhi and its surrounding areas are being witnessed by myself, Zille Ilaahi. The flames of revolution are reaching even the regions of Peshawar, Lahore, and the western territories."

Azimullah Khan - "The Nizam of Hyderabad may be in league with the Britishers, but the word has reached even those among his officials and military commanders who remain loyal to our nation. They, too, are making preparations to the best of their abilities. Thakur Kunwar Singh, Khan Bahadur Khan, Shah Mal, and Raja Nahar Singh have already steeled themselves for martyrdom; they stand poised, waiting with anticipation."

Nana Sahab - "As soon as the revolution begins, Bakht Khan will come to Delhi under your supervision. At this moment, he and his companions are igniting the sparks of rebellion among the Hindostani soldiers in the English barracks."

Ghaus Khan - "Rani Sahiba has also ordered the formation of a force, and work is underway covertly. However, Nana Sahab, an army cannot fight any battle without provisions. What arrangements have been made for this?"

Nana Sahab - "We will make arrangements for provisions through our collective efforts and the contributions received from other kings and princely states, as well as from the pensions provided by the Company. I have brought some funds from my side as well."

Azimullah Khan brought the funds and placed them in front of everyone.

Ghaus Khan - "Rani Sahiba has also sent some funds collected from the moneylenders. (Ghaus Khan opens a mid-sized chest he brought with him) The remaining funds will be spent in Jhansi."

Raja Jai Lal - "For the expenses incurred outside Awadh, the contribution from Begum Sahiba will be delivered to you by tomorrow, Nana Sahab."

Bahadur Shah Zafar - "I have brought everything I had with me. (Pointing) Ahmed Beg!"

Ahmed Beg comes in carrying a bag from outside and a mid-sized chest.

Bahadur Shah Zafar - "All the money I've saved for any difficult times until now is in this chest. (Taking out some jewels from the bag) In addition to that, these are some jewels, our ancestral precious sword from the time of Akbar the Great, and this is my crown."

Nana Sahab stopped Emperor Bahadur Shah Zafar from removing his crown and spoke with enthusiasm and a filled throat.

Nana Sahab - "Let it stay, Alampanah! This is the dignity of all of us and the pride of Hindostan. Let it stay and accept the leadership of the struggle for independence."

Bahadur Shah Zafar - "When the strength of an old father rests in his young sons and daughters, no one can defeat that old father. I accept the responsibility of leading this sacred movement."

Ghaus Khan - "On which date should we choose to commence the fight for independence?"

Nana Sahab - "The rainy season will be favorable, as it will create difficulties for the Britishers in their movements."

Raja Jai Lal - "The rainy season will also present challenges to us."

Azimullah Khan - "Indeed, you are correct! This is our homeland, and the monsoon season here will work in our favor. We possess better knowledge of the local weather and terrain compared to the British authorities."

Bahadur Shah Zafar - "Then let it be decided. Just before the onset of the rainy season, we will begin our struggle for independence. May 31, 1857, will mark a new chapter in the history of Hindostan."

Bahadur Shah Zafar took out bread made of wheat from his bag and broke it into pieces, handing each person a piece in their hands.

Bahadur Shah Zafar - "Let each of us hold this piece of bread, made from the golden grains cultivated in the sacred soil of our motherland, and make a solemn commitment. We vow to dedicate our lives to this land until our final breath, to remain bound to it even in death. We shall not find peace until we secure independence for our nation. And in the event of our failure, we shall leave behind a legacy so profound that future generations will draw inspiration and pride, ultimately liberating our homeland."

Hunter –

The morning had passed, and the sun was shining brightly. The English soldiers were sweating profusely, and among them, Reagan was in the worst condition. The intense heat of Hindostan was no less than a punishment for the fair-skinned officers, but their greed to plunder the wealth of this land had reduced them to mere voracious wolves. The sound of a flowing stream attempted to refresh the environment, but Reagan was still wandering in search of his prey. His eyes, scrutinizing the grass and the jungle with precision, seemed to have decided today that he would not return without a hunt. But fate had settled the score for Reagan's sins, and suddenly, a small arrow shot from a crossbow emerged in the air and found its place in Reagan's neck. Reagan, struggling to catch his breath in the elephant's howdah, fell down as the English and Indian soldiers, in a state of panic, began searching for the attacker in all directions. Standing on a high branch, the veiled Kabir had precisely taken Reagan's life. As soon as the soldiers' eyes fell on Kabir, their guns simultaneously fired. However, Kabir had come prepared. He had strapped a large shield in front of him and deflected the bullets, sliding on a rope to disappear into the jungle beyond the spectacles of his adversaries. Kabir had prepared the path of the rope from one end of the water-stream to the other end the night before, and with the rest of the arrangements, he was waiting for Reagan. For several months, Kabir had been keeping an eye on Reagan, and he had learned when Reagan would come to play his hunting game. As Kabir passed through the jungle, like a leopard on hunt, his eyes were moist, but his face was adorned with a faint, contented smile, spreading a serene sense of victory.

1857 –

The time was not far when the land of Hindostan would erupt in flames and the British flag would sway in ashes. But fate had perhaps something else in store. In the past hundred years, as the power of the British was growing, so were their atrocities. Finally, the patience of the people of Hindostan ran out, and before its time, on May 10, 1857, the spark of revolution ignited in Meerut. If the revolution had started simultaneously everywhere at its appointed time, the British rule would have been erased from the entire Hindostan. However, even the storm that came had shaken the foundations of British rule to the core. One after another, regions were liberated. In the Battle of Chinhat, defeating the British, the light that rose from Barrackpore reached Awadh and ultimately reached Delhi, where once again, Emperor Bahadur Shah Zafar ascended the throne of Hindostan. Nana Sahab declared himself the deputy of the emperor and the commander-in-chief, and Kanpur began breathing the air of freedom. Begum Hazrat Mahal took charge of the entire region of Awadh from Lucknow and Rani Lakshmibai of Jhansi, along with General Ghaus Khan, defeated the British one after another. Thakur Kunwar Singh displayed his valor in Bihar and Ballia, while Maulvi Ahmadullah infused new life into the regions of Awadh and Eastern Uttar Pradesh. Tatya Tope provided strong support to Nana Sahab and Rani Lakshmibai. They drove the British out of Sindh, Peshawar, Jatland, Rajputana, and Central India. Even in those regions where the rulers were loyal to the British, the patriots began inflicting decisive defeats on the British. In Deccan as well, the courage of the revolutionaries shattered the sleep of the British.

Kabir now started living in the house of Pandit Ji. Although Pandit Ji's house was small, it was sturdy, and he also had some fertile land. Pandit Ji was alone in life as fate had taken away his life partner long before. After Kabir became an orphan, Pandit Ji's affection for Kabir grew even stronger. They would clean the house together, prepare meals, and sometimes Pandit Ji would lovingly feed Kabir with his own hands. When Pandit Ji would be engrossed in his pooja, Kabir would place his hand on his chest, showing respect and reverence, and would sit behind him. And when it was time for Namaz, Kabir would also perform it. Jasoda didn't distance her Kanhaiya (Kabir) from his ancestral religion; instead, she provided him teachings of both religions and taught him to respect and honor both faiths. Imam Sahab also adored Kabir very much. He would often come to see him, sometimes bringing vegetarian food and together they would become companions in each other's solitude. During those times, this was a beautiful example of love, affection, camaraderie, and unity, while society did not lack discrimination and prejudice. When Kabir would feel disheartened, he would quietly walk to his own home nearby and, with his mother Jasoda's old dupatta pressed against his face and eyes, he would weep softly. Kabir and Pandit Ji would engage in farming on their inherited plot of fertile land, cultivating crops and vegetables. In the evenings, Kabir would make time to continue studying mathematics and alchemy from Pandit Ji and Imam Sahab, and would often review the knowledge acquired in the laboratory.

January 1858 –

The fourth quarter of the day had already started, the sky was covered with clouds, and a gentle breeze was blowing despite the cold weather. The mustard crop in the field was swaying with the wind, as if a beautiful woman was playfully teasing her beloved, swaying, fluttering, and shaking her head in denial over something he said. On that day, Kabir was working alone in the field, and as he was mending the water ways, his mind swiftly shifted towards the approaching sound of a fast-moving closed English buggy coming towards the village. A

Britisher was forcefully whipping the horses and speeding towards the field. The buggy was just a short distance away from the field when its wheel got stuck in a pothole, causing the buggy, along with the horses, to overturn due to its speed. Due to the intense impact of the fall, the harness from which the horses were pulling snapped forcefully, and the horses themselves became so startled by the fall that they panicked and broke free in different directions, causing the reins to break and scatter in various directions. The fortunate streak didn't continue for the buggy driver. As the buggy overturned, due to the reins getting entangled, he ended up falling near the buggy itself, with one of his hands getting trapped underneath the next section of the buggy. Pain and anguish caused him to let out a scream.

As soon as Kabir attempted to rush to help, he hesitated for a moment as he saw a British girl swiftly emerging from the overturned buggy. The girl exerted all her strength to pull the British buggy driver's hand out, but it was beyond the capability of her delicate body. Kabir quickly moved forward to offer his assistance. However, before he could reach the scene, the buggy driver let out a loud scream,

Buggy Driver - "Run, Alizi run! Hide and save yourself."

The girl swiftly lifted her skirt and sprinted, finding refuge in a nearby field. In a matter of moments, a series of events unfolded: the cart overturned, the horses bolted, the Buggy Driver's hand became trapped beneath the cart, and Alizi made her escape and concealed herself. These incidents transpired in mere seconds. Amidst the chaos, Kabir also sought aid. While Kabir had witnessed Alizi's retreat into the fields, she remained unaware of his presence. Kabir strained with all his might to assist Baghivan (Buggy driver), crying out for help as he struggled. Regrettably, his calls for assistance fell upon deaf ears, and Kabir couldn't free the Englishman's hand from under the cart.

The entire scene echoed with the thunderous hoofbeats of horses. Approximately 15-20 Tilange (British-Indian rebel soldiers) riders appeared to be in pursuit of the same Englishman. Kabir advanced and implored assistance from one of the soldiers.

Kabir (with a trembling voice) - " Brother, please lend a hand, or else his life is at risk."

Tilanga Soldier (with anger and hatred) - "Step back! You're helping the foreigner? Either you're a traitor or a fool!"

The soldier pushed Kabir forcefully, causing him to fall back, and then all the riders pounced on the defenseless Englishman. Whoever got the chance struck him, and no one gave the firangi an opportunity for self-explaination or tried to free his trapped hand. Kabir had never witnessed such inhumanity from his fellow countrymen before. He had always believed that these firangis were the ones who were cruel, deceitful, and heartless. However, today, seeing this savagery and madness among his own countrymen, he was filled with sorrow, anger, and a sense of helplessness. Kabir desperately ran amidst the chaotic crowd, trying to save the helpless Englishman. In the end, he clinged to Buggy Driver with the hope that perhaps if his own body faced some blows, it would invoke mercy in the hearts of the soldier riders. Three soldiers forcibly separated Kabir from the Englishman and continuously slapped him as they dragged him towards a nearby tree, where they tied him up. The oppression had crossed all limits, and another stain of brutality was about to be added to the sacred fabric of the Indian struggle for independence, reminiscent of the massacres in Delhi and Kanpur.

One soldier (with hatred towards the Englishman, shouting) - "Speak, you firangi! Say deen deen, dharm dharm, say! say! say! (Continuing to attack), Allahu Akbar, say it!"

The second soldier (kicking him on the head) - "Har Har Mahadev! Say it, you bloody firangi, say! Ya Ali, Bajrang Bali, long live Hindostan, say it! Say it! Say it!" (With frenzy, grinding his teeth and continuing to attack multiple times).

The third soldier - "Say! May the Emperor's glory rise. Speak! Long live Nana Sahab Peshwa, say it you bastard!"

The soldier riders continued to beat him while shouting slogans of religious and communal harmony between Hindus and Muslims. They forced him to repeat those slogans. The helpless Englishman, gasping for breath, with a broken voice, kept pleading for mercy and repeated the slogans in a feeble voice. Those who claimed to be patriots and bearers of the flag of loyalty to the homeland were tarnishing their own sacred slogans with their hatred and oppression. Whether it was good fortune or misfortune, Alizi found herself hiding in the nearby field, helpless, listening to all the atrocities with her own ears, and being consumed by terror, shrinking within herself. Kabir, bound to the tree, was pleading, shouting, and screaming, desperately begging for the mercy and release of that Buggy driver.

The day had come to an end, along with the life of Baghivan. Darkness had taken hold everywhere, accompanied by the eerie sounds of nocturnal creatures. The wind carried such a tumultuous noise that even demons would be frightened by their own shadows. The rain was pouring down as if the earth itself was pleading to wash away the stains of blood on its surface. One soldier rider approached Kabir to untie him,

Soldier (with arrogance) - "Considering yourself a child we are letting you go, otherwise the punishment for treachery is dreadful."

With no alternatives available, Kabir shrouded himself in a cloak of silence. The soldiers pilfered any valuable items they could find from the cart and, after binding

the lifeless body of the Englishman to a horse, dragged it away. Kabir sat for a long time, holding his head in his hands, pondering over his failure. Suddenly, the image of the girl hidden in the field came to his mind, and he decided to check on her well-being. He entered the field to inquire about the girl's condition. In a state of fear and confusion, Alizi, holding a dagger in her hand, pounced on Kabir like a fierce tigress. Kabir, unable to comprehend the situation, found himself with Alizi's dagger pressed against his throat, while he lay in the mud, fallen like a lifeless piece of wood. In a moment of panic, only one word escaped Kabir's throat, "Friend, friend." Alizi recognized his voice and realized that he was the same person who had been trying to help her companion. In the next moment, she gathered herself, overwhelmed with anxiety and confusion, and sat down on one side, consumed by her own turmoil.
Kabir started making gestures to establish a connection with Alizi and, in his broken English, spoke as they both emerged from the field, saying,

Kabir - "come, safety, come."

Alizi, feeling uncertain, silently followed him, wondering what choices she had. After walking some distance behind him, she suddenly turned around and started running towards the direction of the buggy. Kabir, taken aback by this sudden change, became flustered and muttered to himself,

Kabir - "This fair skin will get me killed!"

Kabir, running behind Alizi, was also calling out to her.

Kabir (in a loud voice) - "Hey! Stop, o you trouble! If someone sees us, it will be very bad. Stop, halt!"

Alizi swiftly entered the cart like an arrow and emerged with a bag in her hand. When Kabir saw Alizi coming back towards him, a wave of relief rushed through him, and he blurted out without any reason,

Kabir - "what in bag?"

Alizi, without giving any response, continued to walk with a gaze filled with sadness, looking down at the ground. Kabir understood that he had asked the wrong question, so he also moved forward, leading the way in silence towards the village. Kabir was constantly mindful of the need to remain unseen by anyone.

The tired Panditji entered the house and took a seat on a cot. Kabir quickly prepared a clay pot and brought water in a pitcher. Just as Panditji was about to take a sip of water, Alizi stepped forward as directed by Kabir. Upon seeing an English girl in his house, Panditji choked on the water, causing it to spill down his throat.

Panditji (coughing in anxiety) - "You foolish boy! What trouble have you brought upon us? If someone sees her, the mark of betrayal will be stamped upon our forehead, and whatever is meant to happen will happen to her (pointing towards Alizi with his finger), but the revolutionaries will hang us too on the neem tree outside."

Kabir (in a questioning tone) - "The soldiers ruthlessly murdered her companion. Is this what the fight for freedom has come to? And Guruji, what should we do? Should we abandon her to the mercy of those untrustworthy so-called patriots for her destiny?"

Panditji (hesitant) - "No! You did a great job

by saving her life, but you should have shown her the path towards the English army camp. What was the need to bring her home?"

Kabir - "How would she have managed to get there, Guruji?"

Panditji's mind was now under his control, and he was beginning to realize the potential error in his statement. He placed his hand on Kabir's head and said,

Panditji - "You have done a virtuous deed, my child, and you are right. Arrange for her to stay in the innermost room. I will bring Imam Abdur-Rahman with me. We must find a permanent solution to this issue."

Pandit Ramdas quickly summoned Imam Abdur-Rahman. Imam Sahab entered the house, expressing his surprise at Panditji's urgency and commotion.

Imam Sahab - "What catastrophe has befallen at such a late hour, Pandit? That you seem so agitated?"

Pandit ji - "Sit down, cool your mind a bit (offering the water jug forward), then I will tell you."

Imam Sahab had only taken two sips of water when he noticed Alizi standing at the far end of the house. The water got stuck in his throat, and he too began to choke,

Imam sahab (patting his chest to ease the water down and coughing) - "La hawla wala quwwata! What epidemic have you brought into the house, fool! (looking at Kabir and questioning)"

The Imam Sahab was asking questions to Kabir, but he was receiving answers from Pandit Ji.

Pandit Ji - "In the evening, some deceitful so-called nationalists senselessly murdered an innocent British man, and this girl was with him. She had hidden herself to save her life and honor. Poor thing! Kabir brought her along to ensure her safety."

Imam Sahab (with a slight smile on his face) - "MashaAllah, my child! You have done a noble deed. But why not show her the path towards an English military camp? Was it necessary to bring her home?"

Pandit Ji - "Could she have made it there alone? On the way, she would encounter all sorts of unknown individuals who could have jeopardized her safety. Moreover, it would have tarnished the centuries-old sacred culture of this land."

Imam Sahab expressed regret over his previous statement as he embraced Kabir and said,

Imam Sahab - "Well said, Pandit. Providing refuge to the oppressed is the humanitarian and religious duty of every individual. You have done a courageous and wise deed, my child." (Imam Sahab gazes at Kabir with teary eyes)

Pandit Ji - "Now, suggest a route through which she can be safely and securely escorted to her people, ensuring her protection and well-being."

Imam Sahab, while sitting on the cot, pondered for a moment and then said,

Imam Sahab - "Let some time pass, let the atmosphere cool down a bit, and then she will be safely escorted. It's not a difficult task."

Pandit Ji (with a hint of frustration) - "How can it not be a difficult task? The moment she steps out of the house, her fair skin will scream out her English origins, announcing it to the surrounding villages."

Imam Sahab - "Oh brother! If I were to take my own niece somewhere, would people object to that as well?"

Pandit Ji - "Were you born in England, Imam Sahab? (sarcastically)"

Imam Sahab - "No! But my niece is a veiled lady."

As the realization dawned upon Imam Sahab's wisdom, relief spread across the faces of Pandit Ji and Kabir, accompanied by smiles. Meanwhile, Alizi, standing in a corner, observed everything silently, taking in every word and gesture.

Not a morsel of food could go down Alizi's throat. Her eyes watered, but her patience was stronger than the Himalayas. The tears moistened her gaze, but her dignity prevented them from cascading down her cheeks. Imam Sahab and Pandit Ji, observing Alizi's state, desired to offer her comfort from the depths of their hearts. Yet, they hesitated, unsure of how to console a young woman from an unfamiliar community with whom they couldn't even communicate effectively. How could they provide solace to her in such circumstances? Kabir could engage in broken English conversation, but he also lacked the experience of providing reassurance or consolation in such moments. In the room, a large mat was spread on the floor, and everyone was attempting to eat a few morsels slowly. Alizi abruptly jerked her head as if she was making a firm declaration to herself, saying, "No! No more sadness." She swiftly began eating the vegetable curry and chapati that had been served on her plate. When Imam Sahab witnessed this transformation, words of compassion escaped his lips.

Imam Sahab - "Be patient, my daughter! Allah is the ultimate healer; He will set everything right."

Imam Sahab momentarily forgot Alizi's English background and conveyed his regret in Hindostani. Yet, the response he received from Alizi left everyone utterly astonished.

Alizi - "Yes."

The individuals present there were not certain whether Alizi would understand the conversation in Hindostani. Pandit Ji, taken aback, asked in astonishment,

Pandit Ji - "Daughter! Do you understand Hindostani language?"

Alizi - "Yes."

Kabir - "How? You should have spoken earlier!"

Alizi looked at Kabir intently for a moment, then turned towards Imam Sahab and Pandit Ji and addressed them, saying,

Alizi - "I am of British descent, but by birth, I am Hindostani."

Pandit Ji - "I didn't understand, my child."

Alizi - "My father is a British officer; I mean he was (Alizi's eyes welled up) and my mother belonged to a distinguished Hindostani family. I was born right here in

Hindostan, in Banaras."

Imam Sahab (hesitant) - "So, was that carriage driver your father?"

Alizi (in a soft voice) - "Yes."

Pandit Ji - "In this turmoil, where were you risking your lives to go?"

Alizi - "We were going to Delhi."

Imam Sahab - "For what purpose?"

Alizi - "My father consistently opposed the injustices and exploitation perpetrated by the East India Company on the common people of Hindostan. He always voiced his concerns about the Company's treatment of Indian nawabs, kings, and ordinary citizens, fighting for their rights."

Alizi paused for a moment, moistened her throat with a nearby glass of water, and continued speaking,

Alizi - "After the defeat of the revolutionaries in Delhi, the East India Company captured Emperor Bahadur Shah Zafar and is now preparing to bring charges against him for rebelling against the

Company. When my father learned of this, he decided to support Baadshah Salamat. That's why we were going to Delhi."

Pandit Ji - "A trial! What trial will they hold? Monstrous! How can an Emperor rebel against his own country?"

Alizi - "That was also my father's argument, that the company was working in Hindostan as Diwan of the Mughal Empire, and no Diwan can accuse his own emperor of rebellion in his own kingdom. He believed that the company should have conducted trade honestly from the beginning, rather than interfering in the internal affairs of Hindostan."

Alizi, her fresh wounds aggravated by those parting words, struggled to speak through her emotions. Imam Sahab felt a deep sympathy for her and gently rested his compassionate hand on her head, whispering, "Have patience, my child, have patience." Pandit Ji was profoundly affected by her pain, rendering him speechless as he silently implored his deity for her well-being. Kabir sat there with tear-filled eyes, silently observing Alizi as she slowly walked away.

In the north of Lucknow –

Inside the English barracks, General Outram occupies his tent, clutching a letter in his hand. His dense beard, air of self-assurance, and an aura of arrogance make his countenance appear as if he is determined to win every battle today. General Henry enters the tent and offers a salute. Outram signals for Henry to sit and welcomes him with a question.

Outram - "Do you know what this is?"

Henry - "A letter!"

Outram - "Yes, a letter! From Governor General of India, Lord Canning. He has ordered me to recapture Lucknow first, then move towards Shahjahanpur."

Henry (with a look of astonishment) - "This is madness! The city is well defended and fortified. Attacking it is a suicide mission."

Outram - "I had explained this, but Lord Canning responded that after the fall of Delhi, Lucknow has become a symbol and a focal point for the rebellion. This city has a king, and it must be captured at any cost."

Henry - "Hence we have been ordered, we do not have a choice. What is the next move, sir?"

Outram – "After three days, under the cover of night, we will initiate our attack on the city. Our forces will be divided into two battalions. I will lead the first battalion, and you will take command of the second. Your primary task will be to oversee the construction of two pontoon bridges across the Gomti River. While the bridges are being constructed, I will provide covering fire. Once the bridges are ready, you will lead your battalion in crossing the river via the first bridge and approach the city from the north. I will utilize the second bridge and proceed eastward to seize Dilkusha Garden. If we succeed in these maneuvers, we will coordinate a simultaneous assault on the city center – your forces from the north and mine from the east – upon my command."

After explaining his plan to Henry, Outram asked - "All clear?"

Henry - "Yes, sir! Let's crush them so that they may never rise again."

Lucknow, on the banks of the Gomti River –

The third watch of the night has passed, but instead of stars, the sky is glowing with the light of fireballs. The cunning Britishers were outsmarting the brave revolutionaries today. In the intoxication of their previous victories, the Indians unwittingly provided the British with an opportunity that they had been experts in capitalizing on for ages. Despite countless defeats over the years, the Indians had not learned from their mistakes. Today, Outram's plan had worked; taking advantage of the darkness of the night and the carelessness of the revolutionaries, the British forces had successfully crossed the Gomti River through the pontoon bridge. Henry was with the attackers from the north, and Outram, moving like a chess knight, had advanced towards the east with his detachment. When the chaos and the news of the possible failure of the Indians' efforts reached Begum Hazrat Mahal in the palace, she sat in her palanquin and headed towards the Gomti River front to take charge of the battlefield. Begum stood tall and proud, with a light dusky complexion, a strong stature, a silent demeanor, and a face adorned with determination, portraying a powerful and strong-willed personality. In her grandeur, even the mighty suns would bow down in reverence to her. A group of women soldiers guarded the Begum with utmost care, trailing her palanquin. Raja Jai Lal, riding swiftly on his horse, arrived at Begum Hazrat Mahal's procession. As she observed his approach, Begum brought her palanquin to a stop. Raja Jai Lal alighted from his horse and offered a respectful greeting to Begum Sahiba with utmost courtesy.

Begum Hazrat Mahal - "What is the news from the battle, Raja Sahab?"

Raja Jai Lal - "A detachment of British forces is approaching us from the north, and our soldiers are facing difficulties in halting their advance. Simultaneously, Outram is also advancing to the east with his troops."

Begum Hazrat Mahal (with a surprised expression) - "Maulvi Ahmadullah is already leading the forces in the east, then how are we appearing weak there?"

Raja Jai Lal - "The number of soldiers and the provisions in the east have become scarce."

Begum Hazrat Mahal - "How did that happen?"

Raja Jai Lal - "A group of Sardars has broken away from the alliance with Awadh and Maulvi, taking away their troops and provisions. They object to Maulvi's leadership, arguing that they have served Awadh for a longer period and, therefore, suggest that one of them should be appointed as the commander."

Begum Hazrat Mahal - "In the battle, the most capable one is entrusted with the command, not the incompetents. If they truly loved Awadh so much, they wouldn't have left at this critical moment."

Begum Sahiba took a moment to think and then asked further,

Begum Hazrat Mahal - "Why did the Northern front become so weak?"

Raja Jai Lal - "We made a mistake assuming that crossing the Gomti and launching an attack would not be easy. But the British took advantage of the darkness and quickly built a temporary bridge to cross the river. Due to some sardars leaving their posts at that moment, there is also a shortage of ammunition and troops in the northern contingent, so we are unable to respond strongly to the British."

Begum Hazrat Mahal - "Hmm! At this moment, we are not witnessing their displeasure but their betrayal. Anyway! I will deal with them later. Right now, who is with Maulvi at the eastern front?"

Raja Jai Lal - "Ghamandi Singh and his soldiers."

Begum Hazrat Mahal - "Take a portion of the stockpiled gunpowder stored in the palace chambers, accompanied by a small detachment, and proceed to assist Maulvi and Ghamandi. Maulvi possesses both courage and strategic acumen; he will undoubtedly devise a solution to contend with Outram. I will personally assume command of the northern front."

As soon as Begum's command was received, Raja Jai Lal hurriedly set out. Begum addressed to Jyoti, the commander of her women's battalion,

Begum Hazrat Mahal - "Jyoti!"

Jyoti - "Yes, Begum Sahiba."

Begum Hazrat Mahal - "The day has arrived for which the brave Uda established this unit of women. The moment from a few months ago still lingers vividly in my memory when Uda, like a lioness, fearlessly confronted the attack on the Residency by the same Outram and his troops. After her husband's martyrdom, with her precise marksmanship, she took down 32 British soldiers one by one, ultimately sacrificing her own life. That fateful day took my sister away from me, snatched my sister away." (Emotionally repeating)

As Begum Hazrat Mahal remembered Uda, her throat choked up, and tears welled up in her eyes. Composing herself, she called out to the entire contingent,

Begum Hazrat Mahal - "I have unwavering faith that today, united, we shall avenge Uda's sacrifice. She was a lioness, and every woman of Awadh is a lioness. As we hunt down these jackals today, they will come to realize that they have invited their own demise by venturing into the den of lionesses."

The entire atmosphere resonated with the chants of "Long live Begum Sahiba" and "May Devi Uda remain immortal."

The Battlefront of the Gomti River –

Begum Sahiba's palanquin has arrived at the banks of the Gomti River. The Artillery commander, Sher Khan, is relentlessly unleashing fireballs upon the British detachment with his formidable cannons called Sher Dahan (Lion's Mouth). His musketeers are deftly loading gunpowder into their flintlock muskets, aiming at the advancing British soldiers, and firing with precision. Behind each musketeer, two more soldiers stand ready, carefully loading bullets and gunpowder into their respective guns. As soon as one musket is fired, the first soldier standing behind hands over a loaded musket to the marksman soldier and starts refilling the empty musket. Similarly, after the next shot is fired, the third soldier hands over his loaded musket to the marksman and starts refilling the empty musket. However, even after such intense retaliatory attacks, the British soldiers are still firmly entrenched on the battlefield. Upon seeing Begum Sahiba's arrival, Sher Khan hands over the command to his deputy and respectfully greets Begum Sahiba. Without wasting a single moment, Begum Sahiba inquires with Sher Khan,

Begum Hazrat Mahal - "Sher Khan, what are the shortages on the battlefield?"

Sher Khan - "We are facing a shortage of gunpowder, and at the same time, our artillery is running low on cannonballs. Despite our prudent use of gun powder, it's hampering our ability to carry out attacks with the necessary force and swiftness. Additionally, the absence of some commanders and their troops has led to a reduction in our forces."

As Begum Sahiba turned around, she caught sight of Jyoti, who had already arrived with crates of gunpowder by her side.

Begum Hazrat Mahal - "With this much gunpowder, the requirements of cannons and musketeers should be fulfilled."

A glimmer of relief appeared on Sher Khan's face, but the weight of worry did not lift from his forehead.

Sher Khan - "What should be done about the cannonballs, Begum Sahiba?"

Once again, before Begum Sahiba could speak, Jyoti was already present with several crates.

Begum Hazrat Mahal - "Sher Khan! These crates are filled with sharp and pointed pieces of gold, silver, and iron. When the cannonballs become scarce, fill the cannon mouths with these pointed fragments. Perhaps they won't take the enemies' lives, but they will inflict such wounds upon them that they may not remain capable of fighting."

Sher Khan (surprised) - "This will empty the treasury!"

Begum Hazrat Mahal (with a reassuring expression) - "When Awadh itself won't survive, what will we do with this treasure? And as for the future, the people of Hindostan and Awadh are so resilient that they will once again rally around this Begum of Awadh and fill her embrace with their unwavering loyalty."

Just like a lioness assesses the herd of deer before the hunt, Begum Sahiba scrutinized the entire battlefield and the deployment of soldiers with careful consideration. Then, issuing her command, she spoke,

Begum Hazrat Mahal - "Sher Khan! Gather all your musketeers on the left flank to strengthen it. Keep the cannons firing with precision, just as they are doing now. Jyoti! Position the contingent of women on the right flank and execute the strategy of the ocean's waves. Initiate the attack!"

Completing her statement, she gave the final order to Sher Khan.

Begum Hazrat Mahal - "Place the musketeers on the left flank mirroring the formation of the women's contingent."

Jyoti positioned the musketeers of the women's contingent in four rows, one behind the other. As the foremost musketeers fired their shots, those in the rear rows advanced, taking aim, while the initial musketeers stepped back to reload their firearms. Similarly, the musketeers on the left flank were also aggressive, forcing the British attackers to halt their steps under the pressure of the revolutionaries. While the cannonballs rained down, bringing a shower of gold and silver, this rain of wealth had turned into a curse rather than a blessing for the British. Falling like hail from the sky, these sharp fragments either blinded enemy eyes or found their mark in their throats, leaving them sprawled in their tracks. When the footsteps of the British began to falter, Henry made a final move. If this move had succeeded today, it would have marked the decisive attack on Awadh. Accompanied by a few British soldiers, Henry maneuvered towards the right flank of the Awadhi forces, keeping a distance. As the distance grew shorter, Henry signaled the attack, and all the guns fired simultaneously. One bullet narrowly missed Begum Sahiba's neck. If she hadn't instinctively reacted in time to shield herself, the bullet would have struck her throat. It was as though she had an eerie premonition of the impending gunshot, prompting her to act swiftly in self-defense. Numerous brave soldiers sacrificed their lives for the sake of Awadh. Recognizing the delay required to reload muskets, Henry and his soldiers rapidly drew their swords, appearing like a relentless pack of wolves. The unexpected assault caught everyone off guard; however, it wasn't long before the women from the rear ranks assumed control.

Jyoti and her comrades stood as a protective barrier for Begum Sahiba. Jyoti's assault on the British forces was as swift as lightning, claiming the lives of numerous adversaries. In such critical moments, even the lioness of Awadh couldn't withhold her roar. Begum Sahiba's scarf slipped from her head, and her hair cascaded freely as she wielded a sword, fighting as if the very manifestation of Goddess Durga herself stood by the banks of the Gomti to bestow blessings upon us, the people of Hindostan. Pressing forward with unyielding determination, Begum Sahiba gracefully leaped into the air, executing a skillful maneuver that sent a British soldier stumbling backward as she used her legs to push against his chest. Swift and graceful, she followed through, delivering a potent strike with her sword against Henry even before her feet touched the ground.

While Henry managed to parry the formidable blow dealt by the 37-year-old woman, he could not entirely avoid its impact, causing him to stagger and fall. The audacious and rapid counterattack launched by the courageous women of Awadh compelled Henry to retreat. The tide of battle had now shifted in favor of the revolutionaries, as the ceaseless barrage of bullets disrupted the coherence of the British forces, throwing their advance into disarray.

The northern front today showcased the remarkable strength of the revolutionaries. The relentless and fierce bombardment caused the English army to waver and lose ground.

Eastern Front –

Ghamandi Singh assumed command of the right wing, while King Jai Lal took charge of the left wing; however, an unsettling silence hung in the air. The thunderous roar of cannons seemed to emanate solely from the British side, occasionally mingling with the impact of bullets and gunshots, breaking the tranquility of Awadh. Amidst soldiers, artillerymen, and marksmen, Maulvi Ahmadullah stood with the tattered remnants of old walls as his shield, his gaze unwaveringly fixed on the obscurity of the night. It was as if a hawk in the distant skies was diligently seeking its prey upon the earth. Majestic and dignified, Maulvi bore a broad countenance, a flowing white beard, eyes accentuated with kohl(surma), a saffron turban adorning his head, a lengthy tunic draping his form, a towering stature, broad hands, and a fair complexion. At the age of 70, he exuded the aura of a courageous dervish, an almost mystical and celestial presence. Amidst the darkness, Maulvi's gaze halted at a particular spot,

Maulvi Ahmadullah (issuing orders, exclaimed) - "Ghamandi! Position the guns 60 degrees to the right, 10 degrees downward, fire!"

Ghamandi Singh shot a sly smile at Maulvi, and that grin was unmistakably visible even beneath his exquisitely groomed large mustache. As he unraveled the Maulvi's instructions, a torrent of countless bullets poured down in unison. A small group of British soldiers, cloaked in black tarpaulin, crept stealthily forward, seamlessly blending their advance into the darkness. The British appeared ready to catch the Hindostani soldiers off guard, yet destiny intervened, abruptly stalling their progress. Maulvi, pivoting as though a prophet, assessed the cannons neatly aligned in three rows. With unwavering authority in his voice, he issued the subsequent command,

Maulvi Ahmadullah - "Move the cannons of the rear row 30 yards back, let the artillery of the next two rows remain intensely active. Subsequently, keep firing the cannons of the third row and the first row continuously until the cannons of the second row also move back 30 yards. Similarly, in the same manner, eventually, the cannons of the first row should also be shifted 30 yards back."

For a moment, Maulvi closed his eyes as if he were seeking a blessing from his Creator, and then he spoke - "We need to retreat at least 700 yards in the same manner."

Though the soldiers hesitated to retreat as commanded, Ghamandi Singh and Raja Jai Lal swiftly prompted them into action. The withdrawing Awadhi army was easily discernible to Outram, evoking a feeling of triumph within him. However, his seasoned intuition was alerting him to the lurking threat. While issuing orders, Outram stated,

Outram - "It seems the enemy is retreating, move forward with caution."

A commander said while gesturing - "This might be a deception, sir!"

Outram - "Yes, I'm aware, but we have received intelligence indicating their shortage of ammunition. We must proceed vigilantly."

Maulvi's forces were in full retreat. By their side, Ghamandi Singh and a group of his companions ignited small fires using Lohbaan, creating a smokescreen that shielded the Awadhi soldiers and forced the barrage of bullets to cease. Outram constructed a makeshift barrier using sand-filled sacks mounted on wooden carts and took cover behind it as he advanced. While the sandbags provided limited protection against cannonballs, they effectively shielded him from incoming bullets. Outram parted through the veil of smoke and pressed forward. As the pleasant scent of Lohbaan faded, he detected the potent aroma of flammable oil. As Ghamandi Singh created the smokescreen, King Jai Lal had drenched the ground with flammable oil, leaving puddles of it in strategic locations. The heightened anxiety forced Outram to flee in panic,

Outram - "Run! Save yourself!"

Maulvi drew his sword from its sheath, lifting it high and then swiftly cutting through the air before bending down, signaling for the attack. The sky illuminated with countless blazing arrows, and the ground trembled beneath the footsteps of the British soldiers. Fire and explosions engulfed the scattered British troops from all sides. Since Outram had sensed the specter of impending death lurking beneath his steps, In the face of retreat, he was the one who took the lead, ensuring the safety of the handful British soldiers in the row behind him. Outram had managed to evade the explosion by executing a well-timed, acrobatic leap, yet the scorching heat of the flames grazed one of his legs.

Maulvi's cunning strategy had dealt a humiliating defeat to the British even on the eastern front. The defeated armies of Outram and Henry stood on the other side of the Gomti River.

The commencement –

The ancient land of Hindostan lay restless in slumber, its fate tugged at by the threads of destiny. Not a single day or moment passed without witnessing some form of political turmoil on this soil. At times, the Indians were outsmarting the British, while in other instances, the British were successfully executing their schemes. Amidst this prevailing chaos, Alizi became an integral part of Pandit Ji's household, entwining herself with each passing moment. With her wisdom, skills and knowledge, she endeared herself more and more to Pandit Ji and Imam Sahab. Alizi assumed a multitude of responsibilities from maintaining the cleanliness of the house to ensuring arrangements for Pandit Ji's worship and Imam Sahab's ablutions. However, both Pandit Ji and Imam Sahab along with Kabir and Alizi herself were vigilant not to allow even the slightest hint of suspicion to reach the ears of those beyond their abode. Kabir had also found a companion in Alizi, with whom he could engage in discussions spanning a diverse array of topics – principles gleaned from various readings, tried and tested theories, mathematics, history, human rights, technology, Quran, Gita, Bible and numerous other subjects. Alizi's education and upbringing, meticulously nurtured by her father, were of exceptional quality. Her knowledge rivaled Kabir's in every subject.

Resting on a cot, Kabir had one hand resting on his stomach as he flipped through aged papers concerning alchemy. Meanwhile, Alizi remained occupied with food preparation, her concern growing due to the scarcity of firewood. She had persistently requested Kabir to gather firewood in order to begin cooking. She also gently reminded Kabir that it was his turn to wash the utensils for the day. Despite her efforts, Kabir remained firmly rooted to his spot. Over the past few days, Kabir had become deeply immersed in a state of lethargy. When questioned about his sudden indolence, he responded,

Kabir - "I desire a couple of days devoid of agricultural or household tasks. I simply wish to relax, read, eat, venture outside, and rest once more."

Alizi said irritably - "Arise, Your Highness! If you don't collect firewood, how will I manage to cook with nothing but the warmth of my sighs?"

Kabir cast a corpse-like gaze toward Alizi before immersing himself in his task. Alizi's irritation was evident as her hunger pangs grew more intense. She had zero tolerance for even the slightest sensation of hunger. Despite being typically composed even in challenging situations, and adept at finding swift solutions to problems, Alizi would rush like a hungry chicken to peck at anything in her path on regular days when hungry. Alizi approached Kabir with determination, tongs in hand, but then hesitated. She realized that if Kabir remained obstinate, it would further delay the collection of firewood, adding to Alizi's burden. She retreated momentarily, hurried to her room, and retrieved the old bag she had safeguarded by her chest, having rescued it from the buggy on that ill-fated day. Alizi extracted a few papers from the bag and positioned them in front of Kabir's gaze. These weathered documents intrigued Kabir. He began eagerly flipping through the pages, each turn widening his eyes with curiosity. Alizi promptly reclaimed the papers and darted away.

Kabir (bewilderedly) - "What is this nonsense?"

Alizi (playfully smiling) - "Everything comes with a price, go fetch firewood first, then I'll prepare the food, and you can keep studying."

Kabir didn't have time to dwell or ponder; those papers had stirred a whirlwind in his mind. He quickly got up like an arrow released from a bow and soon was present with a heap of firewood, ensuring he wouldn't have to leave for some reason. He grabbed the utensils for washing, but Alizi interrupted him,

Alizi - "Leave the dishes, I know what excitement is brewing inside you. Go! Go plunder the treasure."

Kabir (chuckling) - "Did you ever try the formulas and principles written in those papers?"

Alizi - "I know Awadhi and Hindostani, not Faarsi."

Kabir (surprised) - "Don't you know Persian (Farsi)? I assumed you might be familiar with it as well."

Alizi (with a hint of regret) - "I had just started learning Faarsi, but then so many changes came into my life that I didn't have the time."

Kabir - "Whose documents are these? They appear to be from some sort of laboratory!"

Alizi - "My grandfather passed these papers to my father, and as for their origin and history, please read through them, and I will provide you with the details afterward. I have a general understanding of their contents."

Kabir immersed himself in reading again and hours passed by like minutes.
When Kabir had finished flipping through all the papers, he exclaimed with a chuckle-

"This contains designs for various types of firearms, heavy and light cannons, aerial arrows, also known as 'taghraq' or what the British call rockets, along with techniques for crafting different kinds of chemical compounds and 156 formulas for making gunpowder. Among them, 40 are specifically for rockets!"

Alizi - "Out of these 156 types of gunpowder, the formula for 107 of them is taken from the book 'Al-Furusiyyah wa Al-

Manasib Al-Harbiyah' by Hasan al-Rammah. Hasan al-Rammah was the one who invented the world's first torpedo."

Kabir (confused) - "Torpedo?"

Alizi - "An underwater bomb that floats and collides with ships, causing them to sink."

Kabir - "Oh! Aabi nisf. These papers contain some really interesting information."

Alizi continued - "Out of the 40 formulas for explosives intended for rockets, 22 are derived from the book of Hasan al-Ramah. The remaining 18 are newly developed."

Kabir questioned - "You don't know Persian, so how do you have so much knowledge about this?"

Alizi - "My father conducted in-depth research on these papers; he was the one who informed me about all of this. He even taught me some chemistry. (A faint smile crossed her lips as she remembered her father's teachings.)"

Kabir - "Well, now tell me whose papers are these?"

Alizi - "These belong to the Srirangapatnam's Laboratory."

Kabir - "I don't understand!"

Alizi - "These documents are part of 'Fat-hul Mujahideen,' which were employed by the Mysore army to develop powerful and deadly weaponry. These formulas were used to create destructive and lethal arms, some of which were intended for the development of new types of weapons in the future. However, before they could be put into use, Tipu Sultan faced defeat, and Mysore lost its power. Interestingly, some of these formulas and designs for rockets and rocket launchers were actually created by Sultan himself."

Kabir (in surprise) - "Fathul Mujahideen is a military manual that contains instructions for the army's regulations, principles of warfare, tactics for organizing units, and methods for deploying various weapons. As far as I know, there were no formulas mentioned in it."

Alizi - "Fathul Mujahideen was divided into two parts. One part, which was incorporated into the army, contained military regulations and various tactics. The other part was preserved in the lab of Srirangapatna. The lab at Srirangapatna was dedicated to advanced and high-level research, and every new invention was documented in these manuscripts."

Kabir - "How did these documents end up in your grandfather's possession?"

While speaking, Alizi walked towards the kitchen and took a sip of water from the glass before saying,

Alizi - "My grandfather, Sergeant Stuart, participated in the final battle of Mysore. He held a deep fascination for chemistry. Following the downfall of Mysore and amidst the ensuing turmoil of plundering, as the market swarmed with pilfered items, and the volumes in Srirangapatnam's library were being set ablaze, my grandfather hurried to the laboratory, hopeful of stumbling upon remarkable weaponry or even precious novel inventions. It was in that very place that he discovered these documents, which he concealed and refrained from surrendering to the company."

Kabir - "Why?"

Alizi - "He was a cunning individual. His

intention was to use these documents to create a new weapon and then sell it to the company, so that he could live his future life in comfort and luxury. However, before he could succeed in his plans, he passed away in year 1810. My grandmother raised my father after his death, and these documents were passed down to him as an inheritance. But due to his principles, he kept them as a secret."

Kabir - "Your grandfather did the right thing by keeping these documents hidden. The lower-tier imitation of the Mysore rocket made by William Congreve played a significant role. With the help of those rockets, Wellesley defeated Napoleon at the Battle of Waterloo. If these documents had fallen into the hands of the company, they would have caused great trouble."

Alizi (nodding in agreement) - "Hmm! That's true."

Kabir (with a sparkle in his eyes) - "Do you know? There's a formula for a kind of explosive in this that creates an explosion with just a slight impact."

Alizi (astonished) - "Really!"

Kabir - "Yes, my creative mind is racing with the idea of crafting a weapon using that formula of explosive which can create a powerful impact with just a slight trigger. If this concept is put into practice and integrated into a practical design, it could potentially reshape the outcome of any battle."

Alizi - "Good, very good! Definitely pursue that idea. By the way, while you were reading, I had a small snack to ease my hunger, but it seems like hunger has returned with a vengeance. Come on! Let's eat, it's going to be quite a while before Ustaad Sahab and Guru Ji return today."

After quickly serving the food, Alizi began eating before Kabir could start. After taking a bite or two,

Alizi - "Starting tomorrow, I'll join you in the laboratory. We can collaborate on experimenting with new formulas."

Kabir (pausing the bite of food near his mouth) - "This is quite risky. If anyone catches us, we might find ourselves in trouble."

Alizi - "Quietly, we'll slip out in the darkness of early morning, evading everyone's attention. Leave me there for a few days. I'll assist in developing new inventions."

Kabir - "Hmm! I'll see, I'll come up with some workaround. Don't worry."

A wave of happiness spreads across Alizi's face, and both of them become engrossed in eating their meal.

Pandit Ji and Imam Sahab had traveled to Lucknow for an imperative task, planning to be away for a few days. Imam Sahab had established his experimental laboratory within an old concealed mansion situated on the outskirts of the village, surrounded by dense forests. With caution, Kabir and Alizi ventured into the location during the stillness of the night, defying the piercing cold. A dense fog enveloped the area, and within the room, a solitary bonfire emitted its glow. As they explored the laboratory, an aura of restlessness prevailed, and their glances intermittently turned towards the sky, anticipating the break of dawn to cast its initial light upon the room. In their collaborative pursuit of an astonishing and exceptional invention, they were unified in their efforts. They continued to pace around, taking in the warmth of the bonfire, and then once more they glanced out through the window to assess the duration of their wait. Finally, the urge of the sun to peek beyond the quilted cover of the clouds became irresistible. Light raced eagerly in all directions, akin to an enthusiastic child. Alizi and Kabir swiftly gathered their equipment – a slim test tube, a beaker, a wide-mouthed flask, a heat lamp, a goldsmith's bellows and more. As Kabir retrieved a thermometer containing a blend of alcohol and water, Alizi intervened, retrieving a mercury thermometer from a bag and offering it to him.

With a joyful expression, Kabir exclaimed - "Wow, a mercury thermometer! I had been requesting Guru Ji and Ustad Ji for so long to bring one, but due to various reasons, it never happened and we continued using the old methods. This seems to be your father's touch!"

Alizi replied, "Yes."

Alizi continued, offering advice to Kabir,

Alizi - "Let's revisit the entire procedure once again, so that our work becomes smoother."

Kabir - "Hmm! Read it aloud once."

Alizi begins reading from the copied note,

Alizi - "Using a glass container, measure 0.16 chhatank (a traditional unit of measurement) of 70% concentrated shora (nitric acid, commonly employed in gold refining). Introduce 1 maasha of mercury into the mixture and allow it to sit for 30 minutes, refraining from applying heat to prevent boiling over. The solution's color should transition to a pale green hue. In another glass container, take twice the amount of 96% concentrated alcohol and swiftly incorporate the mercury solution from the previous vessel, being careful not to spill. As the dense and volatile fumes disperse, a white crystalline substance will settle akin to fine salt at the bottom of the liquid. Filter this substance through a paper strainer, first rinsing it with water and then with alcohol. Subsequently, our mercury-based explosive will be prepared."

After explaining the entire process, Alizi asked with eagerness - "So, this will create an explosive that will detonate with a slight impact. But if this is used in a weapon, it will prove to be more dangerous for the one wielding it!"

Kabir (slightly hesitating) - "Yes, that's why we will use this explosive to bring movement to the traditional weapon made of gunpowder. The entire weapon won't rely solely on it."

Alizi becomes delighted with Kabir's farsightedness and intelligence and they both immerse themselves in shaping a thought into a tangible reality, one that would turn out to be a blessing for the people of Hindostan in the times to come. In no time, the mercury-based explosive was ready. When Kabir struck it with a hammer, the mild explosion startled them both, filling them with immense joy. Kabir was astute in theoretical knowledge but slightly weaker in practical understanding, whereas Alizi excelled in measurements, tool usage, and metallurgy. Wherever Kabir fell short, Alizi bridged the gap with her expertise. They worked while giggling, chatting and teasing each other. If Kabir accidentally grabbed a hot crucible or utensil, Alizi would get worried, but she would also chuckle at his clumsiness. Similarly, when Alizi mixed the wrong chemicals together and was startled by the rising fumes, Kabir found great amusement in her mistake. However, he also made sure to keep an eye out to ensure that dangerous chemicals didn't accidentally combine.

♣♣♣♣

The midday hour was approaching, and outside, the birds had adorned the silvery sunlight with their melodies, making it even more beautiful. Kabir was lost in a world of his own, testing his acquired knowledge against the array of chemicals he had nearby. Meanwhile, Alizi was getting intoxicated by the joyful ambiance outside. As a woodpecker moved from one branch to another with rhythmic taps, a mischievous spark lit up Alizi's face. She stealthily moved like a cat, pressed her foot down, silently fetched a cup of water, and playfully splashed it on Kabir's shirt. Startled by this sudden prank and the coldness of the water, he flinched. When he turned around, he caught sight of Alizi's smiling face, which seemed to melt away his initial irritation in an instant. His face now also showed those mischievous emotions, mirroring her own.

Kabir - "Wait! The aura of calamity, the aunt of devils, I will teach you a lesson."

Kabir swiftly held up the water jug and chased after Alizi with determination.

Alizi exclaimed - "No, Kabir, don't do it, it's very cold!".

Amidst her screams, laughter, and giggles, Alizi darted around the room, skillfully avoiding Kabir's pursuit. Her swift movements carried her in every direction, but Kabir eventually cornered her. Alizi closed her eyes, the rapid rhythm of her breaths and her graceful figure combined to transport her into a state of euphoria, reminiscent of a celestial nymph or a fairy. Kabir observed her intently for a few moments, etching that image into his memory before he closed his own eyes. Briefly, he imprinted the sight into his everlasting recollection. After a while, a gentle smile graced Kabir's face. He gently pressed his lips against Alizi's and, at the same time, held a jug of water, letting the liquid flow over both of them. In that instant, he transformed every fleeting second into an indelible memory. When they regained their composure, they hesitated and moved apart as though their hands had grazed a hot surface. Avoiding each other's gaze for a time, their eyes eventually met, and a blush colored their cheeks. Their gazes alternated between evading and locking for an extended period. Whenever their eyes met, they would lower their heads in bashfulness, their faces illuminated by a heartwarming smile.

Legitimate and illegitimate –

The evening of today had brought with it a sense of ill fate. Everywhere echoed the cries of "Kill, annihilate!" and "Don't spare this traitor and his British mistress." In that same open field near the neem tree where Kabir had witnessed the pinnacle of cruelty against his parents, today Kabir and Alizi found themselves in a worse condition, covered in dust. Some revolutionaries, who had been staying in the village in small groups for the past couple of days, were now thirsty for the blood of both Kabir and

Alizi, resembling the angels of death. Those who had the opportunity were venting their anger and hatred, while none of the villagers dared to oppose these armed revolutionaries. Those who had the courage to challenge them faced a similar fate. Among those revolutionaries, the boldest and perhaps their leader, standing nearby, was observing with a smile. After playing the role of spectators for a while, when he advanced, his companions retreated, and as he started dragging Alizi by her hair towards a nearby hut, suddenly a roar spread through the atmosphere, bringing silence.

"Don't you dare, Sarfaraz Khan! No one will touch this innocent girl."

On this day, destiny refused to bear any injustice. Maulvi Ahmadullah personally intervened to halt this unfairness. Alongside him were Ghamandi Singh, the village landlord - Zalim Singh, Pandit Ramdas and Imam Abdur-Rahman. Pandit Ji hurried to tend to Kabir, while Imam Sahab attempted to move towards Alizi in order to shield her.

Sarfaraz Khan raised his small pistol and pointed it at Imam Sahab - "Those who don't hold their own lives dear can dare to step forward."

Maulvi Ahmadullah (in a thundering voice) - "Sarfaraz! Oppressing the innocent is a heinous crime. Stop! And repent."

Sarfaraz Khan - "This is war. In war and in love, everything is permissible."

At that very moment, an echoing gunshot resounded as a bullet found its mark on Sarfaraz Khan's head. Ghamandi Singh had permanently silenced Sarfaraz Khan's venomous speech with the gun, which he had just emptied of its gunpowder.

Maulvi Ahmadullah - "Not everything is permissible in love and war; only that which is permissible should be."

Astonishing -

The courtyard of Zalim Singh's mansion was now transformed by the crimson hues of the sun in the dawn. Kabir lay on the bed in an injured state, surrounded by everyone, awaiting his awakening. As soon as Kabir opened his eyes, his gaze fell upon his Ustaad ji and Guru ji sitting before him. He attempted to sit up with respect in their presence. However, when his eyes landed on the standing Zalim Singh, his face underwent an instant transformation, a mixture of desperation and anger turned his cheeks red and his eyes welled up with tears. Sensing his condition, Pandit Ji spoke up,

Pandit Ji - "Zalim Singh has always been on our side. We only recently learned this secret from Maulvi Ahmadullah."

Imam Sahab - "Zalim Singh used to support the British to gain their trust and ensure that news of any activity reached the revolutionaries. He has used his estates and wealth to aid the revolutionaries before and continues to do so even now."

The anger and helplessness disappeared from Kabir's face, but all these discussions had freshly stirred the pain of losing his parents for him. When his tears didn't cease flowing from his eyes, Zalim Singh stepped forward and embraced him tightly.

Zalim Singh - "I had no idea that Reagan, in his brutality, would take the lives of your parents; otherwise, I would have stopped him, my son."

The environment fell silent, and the silence lingered until Maulvi Ahmadullah and Ghamandi Singh arrived. Maulvi placed his hand on Alizi's head,

Maulvi Ahmadullah - "How are you, my child?"

Alizi - "I am fine, Maulvi Sahab."

Maulvi Ahmadullah, smiling, addressed Kabir - "And how is my tiger?"

Kabir (in a mischievous tone) - "He's licking his wounds. He intends to soon recover and thwart the firangis in your service."

Maulvi Ahmadullah placed his hand on Kabir's head and smiled for a moment, then turned towards Zalim Singh and said,

Maulvi Ahmadullah - "Let's go! Now, let's discuss some important issues."

Maulvi Ahmadullah, Zalim Singh, Ghamandi Singh, Imam Sahab, and Pandit Ji sat down on nearby sofas. Kabir and Alizi could hear their conversation and were also able to comfortably convey their thoughts to them.

Zalim Singh - "Maulvi Sahab, what was the reason behind the defeat in Lucknow?"

Maulvi Ahmadullah - "Internal discord. Zalim Singh, among us Indians, there are many who foster internal discord. Their personal gains often take precedence over the well-being and protection of our nation."

Zalim Singh (confused) - "I don't understand."

Maulvi Ahmadullah - "Some of the leaders had hoped that when Begum Sahiba's rule comes to Awadh, they would be rewarded with high positions without any merit. However, Begum Sahiba completely contradicted this notion. Displeased leaders and officials left Awadh, forsaking their allegiance to Begum Sahiba, while some who were favored with positions under her leadership became intoxicated by their newfound power, celebrating before achieving real success and shirking their responsibilities. As a result, even after consecutive defeats of the British, Awadh suffered from a shortage of ammunition. During the final British assault led by

Campbell, we lacked the strength to stop them. We fought valiantly, won all the battles, but ultimately lost the war."

[The command of Lucknow was handed over to Campbell under the leadership of Outram.]

Zalim Singh - "Where is Begum Sahiba?"

Maulvi Ahmadullah - "She has gone into hiding with her compassionate and loyal ally Raja Jai Lal. Perhaps she has headed towards Nepal to gather support and initiate another campaign."

Imam Sahab - "Now, what should we do?"

Maulvi Ahmadullah - "Campbell's next target will be Shahjahanpur. We need to intercept every provision and reinforcement heading towards Shahjahanpur."

Pandit Ji - "How many soldiers you have with you?"

Ghamandi Singh - "One thousand."

Pandit Ji and Imam Sahab spoke together - "What difference will these numbers make?"

Ghamandi Singh - "Wars are won not by numbers, but by courage."

Maulvi Ahmadullah - "The issue isn't the numbers; the real concern is that every reinforcement will pass well-prepared. While we do possess firearms to match the firangis and we can employ them more efficiently than they can, our deficiency lies in artillery. Our artillery pieces are either cumbersome or have been rendered unusable."

Listening attentively to everyone's discussions, Alizi interjects - "We do have a matching response for artillery as well."

Zalim Singh (surprised) - "What is that?"

Alizi - "Vajra"

Alizi's response piques Maulvi's interest.

Maulvi Ahmadullah - "Explain in detail, my child!"

Alizi - "Together, we have created a weapon with the capability to strike targets at a greater range than any artillery and possess even more destructive power than any explosive."

"Can you present a sample?" - Zalim Singh asked in an uncertain tone.

"Of course. All of you will have to gather outside the village in the open field." - Kabir replied with a sparkle.

After a while, Alizi arrived with a bag hanging over her shoulder, clutching a tube in her hand, and carrying a tripod to set it up. One end of the tube remained open, while the opposite end was sealed. The sealed end of the tube was attached to a broad and flat plate with a pivot, allowing the tube to be placed on the ground and adjusted to various angles. The tube's diameter was approximately 80 mm by today's standards. Taking the bag from Alizi's hand, Kabir cautiously extracted the Vajra from it and presented it. The Vajra resembled an elongated egg, featuring a small lid on one end and a thin tube fixed on the other end, matching the eggular part's length. The tube's final end was sealed, yet at its tip, reminiscent of an arrow's design, were wings spread wide. The wings' width, combined with the tip, equaled the eggular part's width of the tube.

Kabir, with the help of the tripod, positioned the tube at a 45-degree angle. Alizi removed the small lid from one end of Vajra and inserted it into the mouth of the tube from the end with wings, leaving it to fall inside. As Vajra descended, it emerged from the tube with a powerful explosion and went quite far before plummeting. Upon impact, another explosion occurred within it, scattering its fragments rapidly in the air and causing destruction upon contact with anything. This astonishing sight left everyone in awe.

Ghamandi Singh (in amazement) - "Its reach is truly more distant and impact more dangerous than an actual artillery piece!"

Zalim Singh - "What a creation! (widening his eyes)"

Maulvi Ahmadullah - "How does it work?"

Kabir - "Both ends of the Vajra, including the tip of the tube and beneath the lid, are equipped with a small amount of explosive that reacts to even a slight impact. The slender tube and the egg-shaped casing contain gunpowder, with the tube itself being constructed from solid iron and the casing made of cast iron. The bigger tube, which is affixed with a plate, contains an internal pin."

Kabir further elucidated - "When the Vajra is inserted into the tube from the end with wings, the sharp internal pin within the bigger tube hits it at thinner tubular end, leading to a minor explosion. This explosion initiates the ignition of the gunpowder in the slender tube of the Vajra, propelling it out of the bigger tube with the force similar to a bullet. Upon reaching its intended target and striking the end of the eggular casing, it induces a minor detonation in the gunpowder stored within the egg-shaped casing, resulting in the explosive impact of the Vajra."

Everyone was listening attentively, hanging on to each detail. After completing Kabir's explanation, Alizi said,

Alizi - "The wings at the end of the tube maintain its stability in the air and increase its effective range."

Those young individuals had prepared the very first prototype of a mortar shell that is used in today's time, and it was seen in action again for the first time after that in the first world war.

Maulvi Ahmadullah, being impressed, congratulated both - "Bravo, my children, bravo! As long as we have sons and daughters like you on this soil, I am confident that this nation will soon break its chains and rise."

Pandit ji and Imam sahab, with joyful and radiant faces, couldn't help but feel a sense of pride and happiness for the success of their children. Their hearts were swelling with happiness from within.

Sunnat –

It seemed as though the entire expanse of Hindostan had compressed itself within the confines of this humble village; the fervor for freedom was palpable in the very atmosphere. A portion of the village had undergone a transformation, becoming a bustling workshop where muskets and wooden cannons, their deceptive weight belying their true lightness designed to outwit the firangis, were being meticulously crafted. Restoration efforts were in progress on two antiquated, lightweight cannons, while Kabir vigilantly oversaw the allocation of available gunpowder for the creation of the Vajra. In a distinct corner of the village, Ghamandi Singh continued his training regimen for his contingent of 1000 revolutionary soldiers. Simultaneously, on another front, Alizi had commenced the assembly of a determined group comprising village women and girls, all prepared to join the fight.

As Maulvi Ahmadullah surveyed the preparations, his expression exhibited signs of approval. Yet, as he passed by Alizi and observed her unwavering determination, his stride briefly faltered, captivated by her fervent resolve. Alongside the Maulvi were Zalim Singh, Pandit ji, and Imam sahab. Although a smile initially graced Maulvi's face, it swiftly transformed into a thoughtful concern.

Addressing Alizi, Maulvi Ahmadullah advised - "My dear, prioritizing your safety over preparing for active involvement in the war would be wiser. Consider going to the British barracks in Lucknow. Ghamandi will escort you there, given the uncertainty of the war's outcome. God forbid, if you are apprehended, the British might label you a traitor and subject you to severe cruelty.

Besides, women often suffer from compounded hardships during times of conflict."

Alizi (with pride on her face) - "I am an Indian, and I am prepared to endure anything for my homeland. I would request you not to deter me from fulfilling my duty to my soil."

Maulvi Ahmadullah couldn't find any response in the face of Alizi's fervor and determination. He smiled and gently placed his hand on Alizi's head before moving forward.

The darkness had begun to set in, and everyone was slowly moving towards the mansion. Imam sahab was walking with the slowest pace, lost in deep contemplation.

Pandit ji tapped him gently and asked - "What thoughts occupy your mind, Rahmaan?"

Imam sahab replied - "Nothing much, just an incident keeps coming to my mind, which is making me think deeply about Kabir."

Zalim Singh - "Which incident are you referring to, Imam sahab?"

Imam sahab, while mentioning that incident, gets lost in the past -

♣♣♣♣

The congregation had gathered in the village mosque for the Asr (evening prayer), forming orderly rows. Worshipers stood in unison, bowing and prostrating as they remembered their Lord, with Imam Sahab leading the prayer. Meanwhile, young Kabir, just three years old, entered the mosque, completely engrossed in his own world and clutching a small wooden horse. The synchronized movements of the worshipers intrigued the young child, and he curiously approached Imam Sahab, his eyes widening as he observed the prayer leader closely. Seizing the moment, Kabir climbed onto Imam Sahab's back just as he went into prostration once more.

Kabir (in a stuttering voice) - "Come, my horse, tik tik tik."

Kabir's innocence had elicited a smile on Imam Sahab's countenance. For a moment, he contemplated lifting Kabir from his back, yet he soon recollected the tradition (Sunnah) established by Prophet Muhammad (peace be upon him) and the esteemed martyr Imam Hussain (may God be pleased with him). He recalled the incident, where Imam Hussain (may God be pleased with him) would ascend onto the back of his grandfather, the Messenger of Allah, Prophet Muhammad (peace be upon him) during his prostration. The Messenger of Allah (peace be upon him) would maintain his prostration until Imam Hussain (may God be pleased with him) dismounted. Imam Sahab's lips curved into a smile as he continued to prostrate, demonstrating his gratitude to the Almighty for endowing him with the privilege to uphold this Sunnah. When Kabir eventually stepped down from his back, the prayer was concluded.

♣♣♣♣

Upon hearing the entire incident, Pandit ji exclaimed - "You should take joy and pride in this. How fortunate our Kabir is! By eating earth alongside Jasoda, he followed the Sunnah of Lord Shri Krishna, and with you, the Sunnah of Hazrat Imam Hussain (may God be pleased with him) as well."

Imam Sahab - "Hmmm! I fear that Allah might be indicating toward his martyrdom in the times to come."

Maulvi Ahmadullah - "Hazrat Imam Hussain (may God be pleased with him) sacrificed his life for the sake of truth. Even if this was a sign from Allah, the Almighty chose him to be devoted to truth and homeland. Will you deprive your son of such fortune?"

Imam Sahab - "No. (Even uttering this word choked his throat.)"

They were all moving forward with slow steps when Ghamandi Singh suddenly felt like someone was shadowing him. Ghamandi Singh swiftly grabbed the person's collar, drew his sword from its scabbard, and held it against the person's neck.

Stranger (in extreme fear) - "Mercy, please, have mercy! My lord."

Ghamandi Singh - "Who are you, and why are you following us?"

Stranger - "My name is Ghure, sir. I live in the untouchable settlement outside the village."

Zalim Singh (angrily) - "Move away, untouchable! You have defiled my religion. Now I have to purify myself with holy Ganges water."

Pandit ji (rebuking Zalim Singh) - "What ignorant words you speak, Zamindar Sahab! How can anyone be untouchable when all are the offspring of Brahma?"

Zalim Singh - "Even though you are a Brahmin, what kind of words are you speaking, Pandit ji? The caste system has been created by the Divine."

Pandit ji - "A person's worth is not determined by their birth but by their efforts. No task is insignificant or superior; each holds its own importance in society. If Shabari were an 'achhoot' (untouchable), Lord Shri Ram wouldn't have eaten the berries she offered. Similarly, if work were classified as small or large, Lord Shri Krishna wouldn't have herded the cows."

Pandit ji's response had made Zalim Singh realize the fallacy in his perspective, and his bowed head was a testament to this realization.

Ghamandi Singh (with a stern look) - "Why did you arrive here?"

Ghure - "I haven't eaten anything for several days. In this chaos and turmoil, no one in the settlement has anything to eat."

Maulvi Ahmadullah - "Zalim Singh, you need to organize provisions for food, drink, and other essentials for him and the inhabitants of his settlement. Ghamandi! it's your responsibility to ensure suitable employment opportunities for them."

Maulvi Ahmadullah then asked Ghure - "Will you and your people fight against the British on our behalf?"

Ghamandi Singh - "I doubt these people would be capable of fighting, Maulvi."

Maulvi Ahmadullah - "You are forgetting, Ghamandi. Those whom we considered untouchables turned out to be excellent soldiers. They fought for the British and defeated Peshwa Bajirao II's forces in the Battle of Bhima Koregaon."

Maulvi Ahmadullah asked Ghure once again - "Would you stand by our side?"

Ghure - "Why wouldn't we? Our forefathers rest in this very soil. We hold this nation as dearly as you do. It's only when someone disowns their own that they turn to others. Otherwise, who abandons their own and their homeland, sir?"

Alongside Ghure, nearly 100 revolutionary men joined, and with Alizi, around 100 more women and girls increased the count of revolutionaries to 1200.

Surprise -

General Campbell assumed command of the British forces in Lucknow, raising the British flag, while Outram supervised the operation. To address the turmoil in Shahjahanpur, immediate provisions and reinforcements were dispatched. As the British contingent advanced across the region between the Ganges and Yamuna rivers, it comprised around 5000 soldiers equipped with their portable cannons, making rapid headway. A scout, assigned to precede Brigadier General Jones, promptly returned with information.

Soldier - "Sir! A thousand to twelve hundred strong army is standing four miles ahead. They are in formation and ready to block us."

Brigadier General Jones asked his deputy in a firm voice - "Sergeant! Is there any way around, can we bypass them?"

Sergeant - "No, sir!"

Brigadier General Jones - "Move ahead in battle formation."

Finally, Brigadier's troops encountered Maulvi's forces. Even in the month of April, the sun was scorching in the sky, and the earth was being roasted like a copper plate. The shimmering heat prevented anyone's gaze from lingering on the ground. Maulvi's soldiers had constructed small mounds of earth, shielding themselves, while two lightweight cannons were positioned up front under the command of Zalim Singh. Under the command of Ghamandi Singh on the right flank and under Ghure's leadership on the left, the marksmen were stationed. Wooden dummy cannons were strategically placed far behind the firing line of the British troops to mislead their artillery shots. The aroma of gunpowder permeated the air, initially stirred by the hands of the Hindostani soldiers. Both cannons commenced firing incessantly, and the elevated mounds provided cover for the musketeers as they advanced gradually. Ghure was stepping onto the battlefield for the first time, yet Ghamandi Singh had prepared him thoroughly. The retaliatory response to the British gunfire also began to gain effectiveness, as the bombardment from the British cannons, being more numerous, took a toll on the Maulvi's soldiers and artillery. Nonetheless, the soldiers under the Maulvi's command continued their advancement. While observing the simultaneous progress of both wings of the Hindostani forces, the Brigadier's forehead bore lines of concern.

Brigadier General Jones (in astonishment) - "Are they mad? Target them with cannons and move our soldiers ahead, pound them hard!"

As the British soldiers advanced, the gunfire intensified, and Ghamandi and Ghure swiftly withdrew under the mounting pressure, almost as if they had anticipated this moment.

Sergeant (with enthusiasm) - "Pound them harder! We will overwhelm them and seize their cannons."

Brigadier General Jones (with a sense of danger) - "They have enough cannons, still they are not using them. This must be a trap, like Lucknow."

Sergeant - "But sir, we can't keep standing here all day long."

Brigadier General Jones (with a sense of danger) - "Keep a safe distance, scan for any traps."

The British soldiers had advanced considerably, pressuring the Hindostani soldiers. However, Jones stopped and examined Maulvi's strategy through his binoculars. He had no alternative but to advance, as choosing another path would allow Maulvi and his troops into an offensive, and an attack from a different direction would inflict substantial damage.

Jones meticulously observed the area under Maulvi's command but failed to spot Kabir and Alizi's troops, who were strategically positioned in ground-level trenches armed with Vajra. Suddenly, on Maulvi's order, Ghure signaled loudly by blowing the turturi, and simultaneous bombardment from both the trenches started wreaking havoc on the British forces. Jones and his soldiers were left in a state of confusion as they faced explosions in the open field without being able to locate any cannons. In a matter of moments, the British dream of conquering Shahjahanpur crumbled to dust. Jones and the surviving soldiers managed to escape with their lives.

In the next few days, many provision and reinforcements of the Britishers were repeatedly decimated, and no Britisher could comprehend the secret of explosions that shattered the ground without the presence of cannons. This mystery had also sown fear among the high-ranking English officers in their grand camps, alongside their soldiers.

♣♣♣♣

General Colin Campbell, chastising his officers in the English camp - "How the hell are you guys being defeated by that old fool repeatedly?"

Brigadier General Jones, while giving his report - "Sir! He is using invisible weapons. How do we counter that?"

A nearby officer speaks up - "Sir! I believe he possesses mystical abilities. Otherwise, how can he maneuver his army so swiftly? He seems to materialize from any direction, and we never witness real cannons in action."

In support to the officer's statement, a soldier, brimming with confidence, says - "Sir! Indians say that he is an Aamil (Muslim sufi with magical powers) and controls many muwakkils (supernatural beings) and angels."

"Not angels, he must be having a pact with the devil," - the officer replied, reassured by the soldier's words.

"Stop this nonsense! All of you are terrified idiots. If none of you have the guts to defeat him, I will tell you how to bypass him." - General Colin Campbell said angrily.

The series of British defeats had rejuvenated the spirits of the Hindostanis, and a multitude of rumors further heightened the apprehension among the firangis. Nevertheless, General Colin Campbell's tactical acumen directed fresh supplies and reinforcements not directly toward Shahjahanpur. Instead, they veered southwest before heading north to approach Shahjahanpur.

Trump card -

As soon as the news of the English cleverly bypassing the Indian insurgents reached Maulvi, unease permeated the Hindostani camp. Safeguarding Shahjahanpur was essential to keep the freedom movement alive and lead it to success.

Maulvi asked angrily Zalim Singh - "Why haven't we received news about Campbell's march?"

This mistake was going to be very costly, and Zalim Singh was well aware of it.

Zalim Singh (regretfully) - "Given that our allies were situated within the English camp, it is possible that Campbell was aware of this fact, which is why he kept the timing and direction of their march a closely guarded secret until the very last moment. On this occasion, he personally led a substantial contingent with ample provisions toward Shahjahanpur."

Ghamandi Singh - "Hmm! This means the English are preparing for a major assault on Shahjahanpur. If Shahjahanpur falls, then Bareily will likely follow suit."

Maulvi Ahmadullah - "What news do we have from Nawab Bareily, Pandit Ji?"

Pandit Ji - "Nawab Khan Bahadur has repeatedly given the English a tough time so far. But this time, perhaps the British might break with such numbers and power that Nawab Sahab won't be able to push them back. Nana Sahab Peshwa is also present there to display his valor in the upcoming battle with a force of 4,000 soldiers."

Maulvi Ahmadullah - "Imam Sahab! Do we have the means to carry out a major offensive?"

Imam Sahab - "We have a shortage of gunpowder. To prepare a large number of Vajra, we need more gunpowder."

Pandit Ji - "We just need a strong offensive. After that, if we manage to enter the city of Shahjahanpur, we can prepare for the upcoming battles there."

Maulvi Ahmadullah - "The speed at which Campbell has gone indicates that we may not be able to provide timely and fully prepared assistance to Nawab Khan Bahadur and Peshwa Nana Sahab."

Ghamandi Singh (worried) - "Then, Maulvi, think of something."

Maulvi Ahmadullah - "If Nawab Khan Bahadur succeeds in defeating Campbell, then it's good. Otherwise, we will wait."

Standing nearby, Kabir impatiently said - "What's the use of our waiting when Shahjahanpur and Bareily slip from our hands? Then there will be a need for a big battle, and we won't have the strength to bring it to fruition."

Maulvi Ahmadullah reassured - "Don't worry, my child. Allah is the greatest planner. If Campbell succeeds, he will secure Shahjahanpur and head to Bareily. That will be our chance to launch a powerful attack and capture Shahjahanpur. Afterward, we will be able support Nawab Sahab and seek his assistance as well."

Ghamandi Singh interjected in the midst of Maulvi Ahmadullah's words - "But even for a massive assault, we'll need a considerable amount of gunpowder. Where will we get it from?"

For a moment, silence filled the atmosphere. Then, Pandit Ji's voice broke the quietude and scattered it in the air.

Pandit Ji - "There is still a source from which gunpowder can be obtained."

Imam Sahab (in astonishment) - "From where, Pandit Ji?"

Pandit Ji - "From Afghani."

Zalim Singh (in astonishment) - "Are you mad, Pandit Ji? Afghani has hidden all the gunpowder in Lucknow, how can it be brought from there in these circumstances?"

Kabir (in confusion) - "Who is this Afghani, and what about the gunpowder in Lucknow?"

Zalim Singh - "Afghani is the individual who brought us a supply of gunpowder during the last battle in Lucknow. However, due to a slight delay, he arrived after we had already lost the battle, and the British had encircled the entire area. Unable to find another escape route, he concealed the gunpowder stash in Lucknow somewhere."

Imam Sahab - "Hmm! If we can get our hands on the gunpowder from that stash, then everything becomes possible."

Zalim Singh - "(In surprise) Even you, Imam Sahab? Bringing it from there is impossible."

Listening to everyone, Alizi speaks - "What if an Englishman leads our stash to us from Lucknow?"

Everyone asks together - "Who is this Englishman in Lucknow?"

Alizi - "Not in Lucknow, but right here in front of all of you."

Kabir (nervously) - "How? No, no! It's too dangerous, don't be crazy."

All the people sitting there supported Kabir on this matter.

Alizi tried to convince everyone with the intention of gaining their approval - "I'm not in danger; we just need a little courage. My father, General Joshua, was not only an English officer but also a dedicated advocate for human rights. Unfortunately, the way he was killed must have fueled his daughter's hatred towards the Indians. Lady Alizi, who strongly disapproves of the Indians, can secretly relay a message from Campbell to Outram."

Maulvi Ahmadullah (with love and sorrow in his eyes) - "Despite the unfortunate death of your father, how come you have such a strong attachment to the soil of this country, my daughter?"

Alizi - "Certain individuals with malice in their hearts took his life. Their hostility cannot diminish the quest for freedom, nor can it diminish the lifelong dedication and aspirations of my father."

With an effort to push away the sorrow weighing on her heart, Alizi continued - "So it's settled then, we will execute this mission. Guru Ji and Ustad Sahab, please make preparations."

Kabir, his eyes filled with concern, tried to dissuade Alizi from taking such a risk through subtle eye gestures. In response, Alizi conveyed her determination in the same manner. Given the lack of alternative options, everyone consented to this plan. Both Pandit Ji and Imam Sahab volunteered to accompany Alizi and ensure her safety.

♣♣♣♣

A horse-drawn carriage races towards Lucknow. Pandit Ji, disguised as a coachman with a hidden sword under a sheet beside him, spurs the horses onward with the sound of his whip cracking. Inside the carriage, Imam Sahab sits anxiously, clutching a musket, accompanying Alizi on this journey.

Alizi, smiling, says - "I will manage everything; you don't worry."

In response, Imam Sahab offers a faint smile and nods in agreement. The carriage came to a halt at the city's outskirts due to a roadblock created by British soldiers.

"Stop! Who are you people? And where are you headed?" - An English officer with a stern and commanding voice asked sharply.

In response to the question, Imam Sahab disembarked from the carriage, brandishing his weapons. Observing the arms, the British soldiers immediately aimed their guns at him and Pandit Ji.

"We are going to Lord Bahadur's place with Mehm Saab's carriage?" - Pandit Ji replied hesitantly.

"What, Mehm Saab? Who's in the coach?" - The British officer asked in the same stern voice.

"Inside the carriage, there is Lady Alizi, Lord Saab!" - Imam Sahab replied.

"Why has the carriage stopped, Rahman?" - Alizi pretended to be alarmed, peeking from inside to assess the situation.

When the English officer's gaze fell upon Alizi's beautiful countenance, he was momentarily captivated.

Alizi stepped out of the carriage and approached, wearing a charming smile on her face. She asked again - "Is there any issue, officer?"

Regaining his composure, the English officer adjusted his hat and politely asked - "Who are you, my Lady?"

Alizi, in a somewhat intoxicating manner, replied - "I am Alizi, daughter of General Joshua."

The English officer, taken aback - "Oh! I am Sergeant Patrick. I heard about your father's demise. I am extremely sorry for your loss."

Alizi - "Hmm, he chose the wrong side and I will not repeat the same mistake. I have a secret message for General Outram from Sir Colin Campbell."

Sergeant Patrick - "You can tell me; I will make sure the message reaches him."

Alizi (with a hint of mischief in her voice) - "Isn't it a secret?"

Sergeant Patrick - "I appreciate your integrity, Lady Alizi. You can go ahead."

Alizi - "You are such a nice and handsome gentleman."

Alizi, seated in her carriage, began her journey towards the city. Nonetheless, as she left, she bestowed a smile upon Sergeant Patrick, a smile that appeared to convey her captivation by his affection. After successfully meeting the revolutionary Afghan and loading the carriage with boxes of explosives from his concealed cache, they retraced their path to the starting point. At the city's doorstep in Lucknow, ensnared in Alizi's clever intrigue, Sergeant Patrick allowed the carriage to pass without conducting a search.

♣♣♣♣

Sipahsalar Bakht Khan, Nawab Tafazzul Hussain, Prince Firoz Shah (the grandson of Bahadur Shah Zafar, the Emperor of India), Nawab Khan Bahadur, Azimullah Khan, and Peshwa Nana Sahab had given the

British a tough time in Shahjahanpur and Bareily. Campbell had intended to conduct a decisive battle and ended up descending upon them like a ravenous wolf. On April 28, 1858, Nawab Khan Bahadur, Peshwa Nana Sahab, and other revolutionaries cornered Campbell in the Battle of Bachpuriya, akin to how lions corner a pack of wolves. However, this victory came at a high cost, resulting in heavy Indian casualties, and the city's security was no longer guaranteed. Finally, on April 30, 1858, Campbell and his British soldiers successfully entered the city, forcing the revolutionary forces to retreat towards Muhammadi for regrouping. At this point, both Shahjahanpur and Bareily had fallen under Campbell's control.

2 May 1858 –

Colonel Hale assumed the responsibility of securing Shahjahanpur, while Campbell continued his journey towards Bareily. Hale strategically chose the opposite bank of the Khannaut River for his encampment and wasted no time in fortifying the position. Cannons were meticulously positioned around the camp to effectively thwart potential attacks from any direction. Despite the morning still being young, the eagle had already set its sights on its prey. In the growing quietness, as the Maulvi's aged eyes surveyed the entire area, Kabir and Alizi, along with their forces, swiftly executed maneuvers in response to Maulvi's signal, positioning themselves on opposite sides of the English camps. Accompanied by Ghamandi Singh, Imam Sahab, and Pandit Ji, who were anxiously awaiting with their cavalry, Ghure and his skilled marksmen remained vigilant. They even kept a keen eye on the gentle breeze. When Maulvi Ahmadullah gave the signal for the attack, Alizi and Kabir unleashed a barrage of Vajra upon the English campers. The deafening explosions echoed through the air, once again leaving the English unable to discern the precise origins of the cannon fire.

Colonel Hale (panicking) - "Oh my God! Oh my God! Invisible cannons! Maulvi has attacked with his devil's. Take positions, hurry up!"

The English cannons also began to retaliate in the counterattack, but all their firepower went in vain. Due to the greater range of Vajra, the Indian artillery was severely damaging the English encampments, rendering them virtually defenseless. However, the English cannons were unable to hit Kabir and Alizi's forces despite the continuous bombardment. Now, it was the turn of Ghure's marksmen to work their magic. After the uselessness of the English cannons became apparent, Ghure's soldiers, using large rocks, boulders, and other barriers as cover, advanced and unleashed a hail of bullets upon the British, moving forward with every shot. The British musketeers were already prepared and poised for this kind of assault, but Ghure's expert marksmanship shattered their confidence. This moment was eagerly awaited by Ghamandi Singh, Zalim Singh, and the other mounted revolutionaries.

Ghamandi Singh (in frustration) - "Maulvi, are you ready to issue the command for a direct assault, or are we to linger here for several more lifetimes?"

In the Maulvi's decorated surmaposh eyes, a spark ignited. The next moment, his hand was on the hilt of his sword, his Kanpuriya shoes locked in the horse's stirrup, and the air trembled as he roared like a lion, "Yalghaar!"

The revolutionary horsemen turned the waters of Khannaut red with blood, English soldiers stumbled, and Colonel Hale fled with a few of his guards.

G.B. Melson writes on this occasion - "Maulvi acted like a European in the war."

Shahjahanpur was now under the Maulvi's control. The Maulvi arranged for the repair of the cannons in the city and placed them under the command of Zalim Singh for defensive purposes.

Maulvi Ahmadullah - "Ghamandi! Arrange for a town crier in the city to announce that we need funds for the War of Independence. Encourage as many people as possible to contribute towards their duty to the nation."

Maulvi took a brief pause and continued his statement.

Maulvi Ahmadullah - "With this money, arrangements should be made for the salaries of our soldiers, and the remaining amount will be used for preparations for the upcoming major battles. Ghamandi! (Turning the conversation) What is the news from Muhammadi?"

Ghamandi Singh - "Prince Feroz Shah, Nawab Khan Bahadur, Peshwa Nana Sahab, and other revolutionaries are still taking refuge there. The heavy losses from the last battle have not yet been compensated."

A faint smile crosses Ghamandi Singh's face as he adds - "Our victory has rekindled their hopes. Nana Sahab has put forth a plan for a significant assault, rallying all our strength against the British forces."

Ghamandi's words silenced Maulvi.

Ghamandi Singh - "What happened, Maulvi? Speak something!"

Maulvi Ahmadullah - "Gathering without full preparation is not safe, my friend! And what's the news? Where is Nawab Khan

Bahadur securing weapons, ammunition, and supplies from?"

Ghamandi Singh - "Prince Firoz has arranged for the gunpowder and supplies through his supporters, but it's not sufficient for a major battle. At this juncture, Raja Puwaayan Jagannath Singh has come forward and promised assistance with soldiers and more ammunition."

Maulvi Ahmadullah - "Where did the funds for all these arrangements come from?"

Ghamandi Singh - "The funds have been arranged by Begum Hazrat Mahal Sahiba."

Maulvi Ahmadullah (surprised) - "Begum Sahiba is also present?"

Ghamandi Singh - "Yes! Following the Battle of Lucknow, Begum Sahiba arrived directly in Shahjahanpur, dedicating all the funds she had brought with her for the country's cause. Begum Sahiba has extended her wholehearted support to Nawab Khan Bahadur Khan and Peshwa Nana Sahab."

Maulvi Ahmadullah - "But in recent battles, we haven't heard any tales of Begum Sahiba's valor."

Ghamandi Singh - "Begum Sahiba has played an active role in strategizing for every battle, yet her brother, Nana Sahab Peshwa, has kept her away from the battlefield."

Sultan -

Within the next ten days, precisely on May 11th, a fresh British force led by Brigadier General Jones arrived. However, hesitating due to the presence of Maulvi and his troops, Jones refrained from launching an attack and decided to seek assistance from Campbell in Bareily. When he learned of Campbell's departure with a substantial force, Maulvi Ahmadullah and his comrades gathered all the available resources in Shahjahanpur and set forth towards Muhammadi, where they convened with other revolutionaries. The sons of Hindostan were now in the midst of preparing for a crucial battle that would determine the fate of their motherland.

♣♣♣♣

In a small haveli (mansion) in the modest town of Muhammadi today, several brave sons and daughters of Mother India, all eagerly awaited the arrival of Maulvi Ahmadullah and his companions. Finally, Maulvi Ahmadullah, along with some of his comrades, entered the courtyard. Nana Sahab Peshwa, leading all the revolutionaries, welcomed them.

Nana Sahab - "Welcome, Maulvi, welcome! You are most welcome!"

Maulvi Ahmadullah's face lit up with immense joy as he held Nana Sahab's folded (Namaste Position) hands in his own and said - "Thank you, Peshwa Sahab, thank you very much!"

Continuing his conversation and introducing his companions, Maulvi said - "This is Zamindar Zalim Singh, this is our Ghamandi, and these are our young commanders, Kabir and Alizi."

Everyone nodded in acknowledgment of Maulvi's companions with a slight gesture.

Azimullah Khan - "Congratulations, Maulvi

Sahab, for disrupting the British's night's peace!"

Maulvi Ahmadullah - "We were not expecting your presence, we thought you might be advancing the cause of the revolution somewhere else."

Azimullah Khan (smiling) - "I am the shadow of Peshwa Sahab, wherever he is, there I am."

Maulvi greeted Begum Hazrat Mahal with courtesy and said - "The news of your presence here has brought great relief, Begum Sahiba. We had heard that you had gone to Nepal."

Begum Hazrat Mahal - "There is still much work to be done, Maulvi Sahab, Insha'Allah, together we will bring it to fruition."

Maulvi went on to embrace Nawab Khan Bahadur Khan, and after exchanging greetings with Sipahsalar Bakht Khan, he addressed Prince Feroz Shah - "Insha'Allah! Soon, we will conquer Delhi, and with your grandfather, the Emperor of India, Bahadur Shah Zafar, we will also liberate this nation."

Prince Feroz Shah (with tears in his eyes) - "Ameen."

After everyone had taken their respective seats,

Maulvi Ahmadullah - "Nana Sahab Peshwa! What do we need to do next and how? Being the deputy of the Emperor and the Peshwa of the Marathas, you are now our guide."

Nana Sahab - "You are a conqueror, and you are also our elder, so we have all decided that you should lead us further."

Maulvi Ahmadullah - "No, no, Nana Sahab! Your position is significant and greater. How can I take on this responsibility?"

Nana Sahab (explaining) - "Maulvi Sahab! You are the one whom the British have not defeated yet. Even in the last battle of Lucknow, the defeat of other fronts forced you to withdraw, but on your front, you were victorious. Your fear is not only among the British soldiers but also in the heads of British officers. A reward of 50,000 silver coins has been announced on your head. In such circumstances, if you lead our troops, the terror you inspire will win the battle for us before we even set foot on the battlefield."

Ghamandi Singh - "Peshwa Nana Sahab has a point, Maulvi."

Maulvi Ahmadullah looked at Ghamandi Singh with a meaningful gaze, then turned to address everyone, lowering his head humbly, nodded in agreement.

Begum Hazrat Mahal, advancing Nana Sahab Peshwa's words, said - "Maulvi, it's crucial for this message to reach the people completely: the dawn of freedom is not far away, and its beginning has already commenced in the city of Muhammadi."

Maulvi Ahmadullah (hesitatingly) - "I don't understand, Begum Sahiba."

Begum Hazrat Mahal - "We all wish for you to declare yourself the Sultan of Muhammadi under the protection of the Emperor of India. Form a cabinet as well so that a message can reach to the people that the foundation of Free Hindostan has been laid, and which way they should look now."

Maulvi Ahmadullah (hesitatingly) - "Forgive me for my bluntness, Begum

Sahiba! I have always stayed away from politics. Politics often divides even brothers, and besides, I don't have the experience and capability to decide who should be entrusted with what responsibilities."

Begum Hazrat Mahal - "Don't worry, Maulvi! It's not politics; it's the season of martyrdom."

Nana Sahab completed Begum Sahiba's statement - "As for the matter of the cabinet and who should be honoured with what responsibility, we have already discussed this. You just move forward; we are all with you."

Maulvi Ahmadullah gave his consent after a brief silence.

Nawab Khan Bahadur Khan - "Maulvi Sahab! Shed some light on the upcoming campaign, when, what, and how should it be done?"

Maulvi Ahmadullah (addressing Zalim Singh) - "Instruct Pandit Ramdas and Imam Abdur-Rahman to immediately depart for Lucknow with some men. They should closely monitor every activity there and keep us updated on every development."

Maulvi Ahmadullah asked the next question to Bakht Khan - "How much do we have in terms of provision and ammunition?"

Bakht Khan - "We have a maximum of 15 days' worth of provisions. Nana Sahab Peshwa has 4,000, Nawab Khan Bahadur has 2,000, you have 1,200, and with my soldiers, we have a total military strength of approximately 8,000."

Maulvi Ahmadullah - "Gunpowder?"

Shahzada Firoz Shah - "It should be enough to face Campbell with a substantial force, but after that, we won't be able to stop Campbell."

Maulvi Ahmadullah - "Have you estimated Campbell's military strength?"

Shahzada Firoz Shah - "Approximately 15,000 troops and 25 cannons."

Maulvi Ahmadullah - "How many cannons do we have?"

Shahzada Firoz Shah - "9"

Maulvi Ahmadullah - "What happened to

the assistance from Raja Puwaayan?"

Nawab Khan Bahadur Khan - "He has sent the supplies and ammunition, but it's insufficient. Due to surveillance, He can't openly support us because, in the eyes of the British, He is their supporter."

Maulvi Ahmadullah - "When will the soldier's reinforcements from his side be sent?"

Nawab Khan Bahadur Khan - "Raja Jagannath has promised assistance with 4000 soldiers, but he requests that Puwaayan be made the center of the battle because moving 4000 soldiers from there would jeopardize Puwaayan's security and it would also expose his secret to the British."

Maulvi Ahmadullah - "Hmm! We cannot fully trust Raja Jagannath, and there's no immediate need to make Puwaayan the center of the battle."

Maulvi Ahmadullah, completing his statement, said - "We should request further assistance from Raja Puwaayan, and we will welcome Campbell openly in the battlefield."

Maulvi Ahmadullah declared himself the independent ruler of Mohammadabad and the coronation ceremony was completed in front of a gathering of 16,000 people on May 15, 1858. Maulvi Ahmadullah Shah issued coins in his name, special prayers were offered in temples for him, and sermons were preached in his name in mosques. In his independent and formal rule, Sipahsalar Bakht Khan became the Prime Minister, Maulvi Sarfaraz Ali Jaunpuri became the Chief Justice, Nana Sahab Peshwa accepted the positions of Minister and Treasurer. Other prominent members of the cabinet included Maulvi Liyaqat Ali Ilahabadi, Wazir Khan Akbarabadi, Maulvi Faiz Ahmad Badayuni, and Prince Feroze Shah.

Havoc –

On May 24, 1858, beneath the open sky, even the circling vultures could have sensed the impending thirst for blood, as the goddess of war seemed eager to be sated, and her Indian sons had assembled with the intent of painting this battlefield crimson. Campbell deployed his light and long-range cannons in two rows at the forefront, strategically spaced to allow his cavalry to charge effectively through them. Just behind the cannons, skilled British marksmen took their positions within three fortified sections composed of sandbags on wooden carts. These marksmen were under the command of Brigadier General Jones, accompanied by several other British commanders. Positioned at the very rear in a similar formation was the swift cavalry, poised to charge upon the Indians like lightning as soon as the signal was given. This arrangement and the preparedness of the British forces defied conventional British military doctrine. Throughout their history, British infantry had often proven more effective than cavalry. Perhaps Campbell recognized that the speed of the Indian forces on the battlefield posed a significant threat. However, today, all his strategic calculations appeared poised to work against him.

Meanwhile, within the Indian encampment, an assembly of formidable warriors posed a grave threat to British dominion. Each one of them was deadly to the British army, and here, unfortunately for the British, the entire brigade was present. Sultan Maulvi Ahmadullah orchestrated the assembly of his brigade, positioning carefully selected cannons in the foremost row, commanded by Zalim Singh. Positioned behind the cannons, on both the right and left flanks, Alizi stood ready with her female brigade, while Kabir prepared with his troops too to unleash Vajras. Positioned between Alizi and Kabir, Sultan Maulvi Ahmadullah stationed his marksmen, under the leadership of Begum Hazrat Mahal and Ghure. In the rear, the cavalry units were fully prepared. Prince Feroze Shah and Nawab Khan Bahadur Khan were entrusted with the command of the right and left wings of the horse archer cavalry units. Nana Sahab Peshwa, Raja Jai Lal, Bakht Khan, and Ghamandi Singh assumed oversight of the swordsmen cavalry units. Maulvi Ahmadullah, seated atop an elephant at the rearmost position, maintained vigilant watch over the entire battlefield.

The battle was initiated by Campbell. It was just a matter of his command, and then the new English cannons began to rain down. After quite a barrage of cannon fire, when the dust and smoke cleared, these words escaped from Campbell's mouth,

Campbell - "What a fox! He is out of the range. Move the artillery ahead!"

As soon as the British artillery advanced, a victorious smile lit up Maulvi's face. At Maulvi Ahmadullah's signal, a soldier raised the red flag high. Kabir and Alizi, seeing the elevated flag, surged their forces forward, and a powerful rain of Vajras fell upon the British artillery. The British artillery position was in chaos; they tried to respond, but Kabir and Alizi were still out of range of the new British cannons. Seeing his own artillery in such disarray and to protect his position, Campbell urged his marksmen forward. The British riflemen, with wooden carts shielding them, advanced quite swiftly. As Alizi and Kabir's troops were in danger of facing the Englishmen's fire now, a sudden sight caught their attention: a green flag unfurled high above. With a dupatta fixed atop her head and wearing Kanpuriya shoes, Begum Sahiba roared - "Yalghaar",

Ghure and Begum Hazrat Mahal's marksmen, positioned behind the wooden carts, swiftly retaliated against the counterattack. Kabir and Alizi's troops gathered behind the protective barriers of the marksmen's carts to maintain their assault, with Begum and Ghure's marksmen pushing the wooden carts forward, intensifying their attack. Now, it was Zalim

Singh's moment, as he had stood in silence with anticipation for quite some time. He promptly advanced his artillery, causing the ground to shake under the onslaught of cannons' fire, Vajras' rain and rifles' roar. The English side was marred by shattered cannons, scattered rifles, and lifeless soldiers. Amidst the battle's chaos, Campbell's last resort to maintain his position and rescue his besieged troops was to release his cavalry, who, unafraid for their own lives, would attempt to seize the front section of the enemy's line to obstruct the Indian artillery barrage. Then, with the advantage of his superior numbers, Campbell could endeavor to reverse the course of the battle. Campbell's face was flushed with the looming prospect of defeat, and his eyes reflected desperation. No one prior to this event had possessed the audacity or capability to push him to the precipice of defeat like this.

Campbell shouted loudly - "Charge!"

The English cavalry, eager to turn the tide of the battle, surged forward like arrows fired from a bow, risking their lives. Sultan Maulvi Ahmadullah Shah, mounted on an elephant, kept a keen eye on every move, and news of every action reached his troops promptly. Seeing the English cavalry advancing, a simultaneous smile broke out on the faces of Maulvi's commanders as well as Maulvi's, as if they had been waiting for this moment. This time, a saffron flag was kissing the sky, and Prince Feroze Shah and Nawab Khan Bahadur Khan, with their brave warriors, moved forward, talking to the wind as they advanced, raining down a hail of deadly arrows on the English cavalry. One after another, Indian cavalrymen in rows approached the English cavalry, launching a shower of arrows at them, then retreating behind. Wounded soldiers fell, and the English cavalrymen were drenched in blood. Seeing their wounded comrades falling, the spirits of the British soldiers began to waver. Now, it was time for one final and powerful assault. Nana Sahab Peshwa, Raja Jai Lal, Bakht Khan, and Ghamandi Singh also entered the battlefield to settle the score with the British. Their swords left no room for the British to even think about a comeback in the battle. Campbell was dismayed by his defeat, forced to leave the battlefield with only half of his remaining forces. The British were still superior in the aspect of resources, otherwise they had faced defeats in all other aspects.

Caught with a bad hand –

The aroma of gunpowder hanging in the air was electric. Several revolutionary soldiers, holding torches, solemnly performed the last rites for fallen soldiers on the battlefield, regardless of whether they were their own or the enemy's. In the expansive field, the distant sounds of horse neighing carried on the breeze, and the invigorating freshness in the air sought to envelop everyone. Gathered around a roaring fire, discussions about future strategies were underway.

Nawab Khan Bahadur Khan (with great joy) - "These bloody firangis should now forget about defeating us."

Maulvi Ahmadullah Shah (with determination) - "They don't even need to think about winning against us. They just have to stay in this battle longer than us."

Peshwa Nana Sahab - "The English have no shortage of resources; they practically dominate the entire country. Many of our kings and nawabs are groveling at their feet for their own luxuries. They may lose to us in all the battles, but as soon as our resources are depleted, they will automatically win this war."

Kabir (passionately) - "Why aren't we seeking help from Rani Jhansi? If she joins forces with our army and resources, we can consider it a British defeat in North India."

Peshwa Nana Sahab (taking a deep breath) - "Traitors have brought down the strong fortress of Jhansi. Ghaus Khan sacrificed himself for Manu and Jhansi. May God grant his soul peace."

Nana Sahab took a brief pause before resuming - "We've just received word that Manu has dealt a significant blow to the British in Kalpi. If she joins us in such a situation, it might weaken our position there, which could further strengthen the British. The primary goal of launching simultaneous revolutions in various parts of the country was to strategically divide and weaken the British forces."

Alizi further elaborated on the answer to Kabir's question, stating - "Seeking assistance from distant sources would inadvertently offer an opportunity for the scattered British units in between to obstruct any potential reinforcements headed our way. Therefore, it's imperative that we obtain support from local sources; otherwise, we'll be compelled to capture the heavily fortified strongholds of the kings or nawabs allied with the British."

Begum Hazrat Mahal, addressing the Maulvi, inquired - "What do you think will be the next step of the Britishers?"

Maulvi Ahmadullah Shah replied - "The Britishers' steps are advancing towards us in the darkness of this night."

Ghamandi Singh (surprised) - "What are you referring to, Maulvi? There's been some confidential information, and I haven't been informed!"

Maulvi Ahmadullah Shah (with great seriousness) - "No, no news has come."

"So then?" - Several voices together raised this question to Maulvi's side.

Maulvi Ahmadullah Shah - "The Britishers are inclined to take full advantage of every opportunity. I don't believe that Campbell will sit quietly tonight; he must have set out to retaliate."

Zalim Singh - "Then we should prepare ourselves for another major confrontation."

Kabir - "We have enough Vajras for one strong assault, but for a prolonged confrontation, we'll need to prepare a new batch."

Ghamandi Singh - "If the battle drags on, what should we do, Maulvi?"

The arrival of Azimullah Khan interrupted the ongoing debate in the middle.

Azimullah Khan - "On behalf of Raja Puwaayan, a substantial supply of gunpowder and provisions has arrived."

This gives rise to a unique wave of joy in the surroundings.

Zalim Singh - "Hufff! There won't be a shortage of gunpowder now."

Peshwa Nana Sahab - "Hari Om! Hari Om!"

Maulvi Ahmadullah - "Shukr Alhamdulillah!"

"Should we decide on the next plan of action?" - Nawab Khan Bahadur asked confidently.

"Hmm!" - Maulvi Ahmadullah Shah took a deep breath and remained silent for a few moments before speaking.

Maulvi Ahmadullah Shah – "I will lead a surprise assault on Campbell's army alongside Ghamandi and his forces, driving them back. The rest of you should strengthen our defenses here in Muhammadi with these new provisions."

Maulvi Ahmadullah Shah, outlining future plans - "The support received from Raja Jagannath reaffirms his unwavering loyalty. Thus, following our confrontation with Campbell, Ghamandi's troops and I will move towards Puwaayan within a few days. Our aim is not only to establish workshops but also to secure necessary resources and facilities. In the meantime, your task is to keep Campbell occupied. After adequate preparations, I will initiate an attack from the Puwaayan side, while you all launch an attack from this side. Campbell or any British force will be thoroughly defeated, akin to grains being ground between two millstones."

Peshwa Nana Sahab - "May God grant us success!"

Maulvi Ahmadullah Shah - "Inshallah Rahman!"

"Har Har Mahadev!" and "Allahu Akbar!" - These powerful slogans resonated through the mountains.

Amidst the chorus of crickets and the rhythmic convergence of footsteps, Campbell and his troops advanced stealthily and vigilantly. Perched atop his horse, he gripped binoculars in his hands, his intent gaze meticulously surveying the path ahead, as though an enigmatic apprehension had settled within his heart.

Jones - "Are you having doubts, sir?"

Campbell - "We are dealing with a military genius here, that old man can even trick the devil himself."

Hidden within the dense undergrowth, Maulvi Ahmadullah and Ghamandi Singh maintained a vigilant watch over the British forces' movements. Sultan-e-Mohammadi, Maulvi Ahmadullah Shah swiftly drew the string of his bow and loosed a blazing arrow, piercing the shroud of the night and briefly lighting up the sky. In that fleeting radiance, Campbell came to realize that the old man's wisdom carried more weight than his military prowess and cunning. Meanwhile, Zalim Singh unleashed the cannons, and Kabir and Alizi orchestrated a fiery display of firepower that sent shivers not only through the regular soldiers but also among the officers, evoking grim thoughts of the Grim Reaper. Ghamandi and Ghure's marksmen meticulously selected their British targets. It didn't take long for Campbell and his troops to falter. They beat a hasty retreat along the same path they had come from. Campbell was left astounded by Maulvi Ahmadullah's audacious tactics. Campbell suffered his second consecutive defeat.

G.B. Malleson writes about this incident - "Maulvi was the only one to have dared to defeat Sir Colin Campbell twice."

Scattered Pearls -

On June 5, 1858, the prevailing silence within the English army camp was a testament to their fractured morale. Campbell sat in a chair, intermittently sipping from a glass of wine, ensnared in profound contemplation. The furrowed brows and creases on his forehead vividly conveyed his sense of helplessness. Nearby, the melodious chirp of a Myna bird seemed like noise to him, and in his frustration, he had just reached for a stone to shoo the bird away when Jones, galloping on a swift horse, approached the scene.

Jones (saluting) - "Sir! Maulvi is moving towards Puwaayan with a 1200-strong army. King Jagannath seems to have joined hands with the rebels."

Campbell (in astonishment) - "What! Is this a confirmed news?"

Jones - "Yes, sir, he sent them help secretly."

Campbell (gritting his teeth) - "That coward rascal Jagannath will face the consequences."

Jones - "Sir! This is the right time to intercept Maulvi while he is on the way."

Campbell - "He always keeps a trick hidden under his sleeve; we cannot risk falling into another trap. We will wait for reinforcements from Lucknow."

♣♣♣♣

The walls of the fort were adorned with cannons and numerous well-armed guards, giving strong evidence of a robust defensive arrangement. Raja Jagannath and his brother Baldev Singh were observing the approaching revolutionary forces from a turret. Sultan Maulvi Ahmadullah Shah, mounted on an elephant, was advancing at a moderate pace. To Maulvi Ahmadullah Shah's right, mounted on horses, Zalim Singh, Ghamandi Singh, and Kabir, led their resolute soldiers. Their steady strides raised dust, evoking the image of fragments of a dense monsoon cloud. On the left side of Maulvi Ahmadullah Shah, Alizi was accompanied by her group of trusted soldiers, and Ghure marched with his regiment. As they neared the fort, Maulvi's signal prompted Zalim Singh to hoist a high white flag. The sight of the white flag fluttering in the wind seemed to instill a sense of apprehension on Raja Jagannath's face.

Raja Jagannath (Addressing Baldev) - "Think once again, Baldev, lest this proves to be the last mistake of our lives."

Baldev Singh - "Worry not, brother. We are like the clever crow that can never eat garbage."

Baldev also hoisted a white flag on the fort. From King Jagannath's side, a signal of peace was received as well, which brought a sense of relief to Maulvi and his companions.

The distance between Maulvi and the fort had drastically shortened. Sinister smiles suddenly crept onto the resolute faces of Baldev and Jagannath. In unison, the cannons erupted into thunderous volleys, while bullets rained down, claiming the lives of several revolutionaries in an instant. The elephant's valiant mahout courageously shielded Maulvi, sacrificing himself and repaying a debt of loyalty. Without the mahout's guidance, the elephant panicked, darting aimlessly in all directions. In his elderly state, Maulvi struggled to regain control. Bullets peppered the area around the revolutionary forces. As another shell burst before it, the panicked elephant reversed course and sprinted back toward the fort. Undeterred by the life-threatening situation, the revolutionaries decided to counterattack amidst the relentless hail of bullets. Kabir and Alizi rallied their soldiers with resounding cries.

Kabir (in a resounding voice) - "The season of martyrdom has arrived, comrades. Today, let us do everything in such a way that future generations always take pride in us."

Alizi (roaring) - "Brave women of my country! Today, it's a battle to be remembered for ages to come."

Amid the cover of deceased horses and human corpses, Alizi and Kabir's forces rapidly exhausted their remaining Vajras, resulting in the destruction of several fort towers and their defenders. Meanwhile, the madness of a charging elephant possessed Zalim Singh and Ghamandi Singh as they redirected their guns towards the enemy. Ghure, displaying incredible agility, arranged several carts brought with him in a defensive line, and in this endeavor, many soldiers paid the ultimate price of martyrdom. While attempting to place the last cart, a searing bullet found its mark in Ghure's leg. Kneeling on the ground, he was in imminent danger of falling victim to the next bullet. Zalim Singh was not ready to accept such a cheap martyrdom of his compatriot and courageous brother, he hoisted Ghure onto his shoulders and dashed forward, eliminating an enemy soldier stationed on the fort's ramparts with his firearm. However, destiny favored the traitors of the nation on this day, as a stray shell from the fort landed perilously close to Zalim Singh, ending both of their lives. With his brother on his shoulders, Zalim Singh's fall was akin to a massive boulder dislodging itself from the Himalayas. This awe-inspiring sight ignited renewed fervor among the surviving revolutionaries. On the opposite side, Maulvi Ahmadullah Shah, mounted on the distressed elephant, had initially sought refuge behind a robust shield to protect himself from the bullets. However, even this shield had begun to

succumb, and several bullets had already found their mark on his body. The armor covering the fatigued and restless elephant too was riddled with holes, and blood flowed from numerous wounds.
Seeing the revolutionary soldiers still holding their ground, Baldev's anger and frustration reached the seventh heaven,

Baldev - "Haaaaaah!", he grabbed a soldier's rifle and discharged it.

The bullet spun through the air, passing through Alizi's head, who was fighting like a thunderbolt, striking down her enemies. Fate granted her no opportunity to scream or cry; she plummeted to the earth like a falling meteorite. This horrifying spectacle drove Kabir to madness. He abandoned everything and, upon reaching Alizi's side, her wide-open eyes left Kabir paralyzed for a moment. He knelt there for a while, gazing at the sky with an unfeeling stare. Then, it appeared as though a fire had been ignited within him. With bloodshot eyes and clenched fists, he seized a sword and raced toward the fort's bastion. By this point, the revolutionaries had exhausted their ammunition. Ghamandi Singh and a handful of surviving soldiers armed with swords and ropes charged alongside Kabir towards the fort's wall, braving bullets hitting their chests. Ropes were thrown one by one, and Kabir, Ghamandi Singh, and a few others began scaling the broken walls whose defenders lay lifeless. Observing the revolutionaries approaching so closely to the fort, Maulvi cast aside his shield, took an elephant hook in hand, and directed the elephant toward the fort's gates. As the revolutionaries drew near to the fort, Raja Jagannath's senses abruptly flew away.

Raja Jagannath (shouting in fear) - "Baldev! I had said that this might be our last mistake."

Terrified, Raja Jagannath, accompanied by some soldiers, ran and locked himself in a room in the upper part of the fort. But Baldev was made of different material than his brother.

Baldev (issuing orders) - "None of them should survive."

Some soldiers swiftly ran towards that side of the fort's wall and took aim from above. One by one, the remaining revolutionary soldiers sacrificed their lives willingly. Two bullets struck Kabir and Ghamandi Singh's chests simultaneously. Both fell instantly, shattered like fallen leaves, and closed their eyes in the lap of Motherland.

On the other hand, the elephant's powerful charge had shattered the fort's gates like a deck of cards. As he entered, Maulvi Ahmadullah Shah raised the rifle he had kept in the howdah and tried to take Baldev, who was standing above the fort, into his aim. But Baldev, already prepared, stood firm. The last bullet that came out of Baldev's rifle scattered one of the strong pillars of the fortress of independence. The wounded tiger, terrifying the entire forest with its roar, collapsed to the ground and met its martyrdom.

G.B. Melson writes at this moment - "Thus dies the Maulvi Ahmadullah Shah of Faizabad. If a patriot is a man who plots and fights for independence, wrongfully destroyed for his native country, then most certainly, the Maulvi was a true patriot."

♣♣♣♣

After the martyrdom of Maulvi Ahmadullah Shah, Baldev Singh presented his revered head to Collector Mr. G.P. Maane of

Shahjahanpur. Initially, the British found it unbelievable, but their subsequent elation knew no bounds. They displayed Maulvi Ahmadullah's head at the entrance of the Shahjahanpur police station and put his body to fire. This cruel act by the British vividly underscored their humiliation and frustration due to their repeated defeats. The East India Company rewarded Raja Jagannath and Baldev Singh with 50,000 silver coins for their treachery and sold souls. The city's inhabitants could not endure this degradation of their leader, prompting some valiant individuals to launch an attack on the police station. They recovered Maulvi's esteemed head and accorded him a dignified burial on the Khannaut River's banks, within the precincts of the Ahmadpur Masjid, as a mark of profound respect and honor.

The revolutionaries in Muhammadi gathered all their strength to seek retribution for this betrayal and launched a final assault on Puwaayan on October 8, 1858 but combined forces of Raja Jagannath and Campbell thwarted this endeavor. By this time, the defeat of the Indians was complete in every corner of the country. After the last battle, Nana Sahab Peshwa and Begum Hazrat Mahal moved to Nepal, hoping for an opportunity to rekindle the flames of freedom. However, their dream remained unfulfilled throughout their lives.

In the present day, with our nation targeted by enmity and having already endured the repercussions of the British-instigated partition, our duty is heightened. We must strengthen our democracy and commemorate both the renowned and unsung martyrs who demonstrated Hindu-Muslim unity and instilled in us the willingness to sacrifice for this land.

♣♣♣♣

"And never think of those who have been killed in the cause of Allah/duty as dead. Rather, they are alive, with their Lord, receiving provision." - **Quran 3:169**

YOUR REVIEW IS PRECIOUS

www.ingramcontent.com/pod-product-compliance
Lightning Source LLC
LaVergne TN
LVHW041217150826
845673LV00001B/440

* 9 7 9 8 8 9 1 8 6 1 7 6 3 *